Bound in Blue

It was the most glorious of situations: bent across a rusting tractor in the countryside with my trousers pulled down and a man's penis swelling in my mouth. Perhaps it should have been some rough and ready farmhand instead of my caring, gentle Robert, but his cock was every bit as good. It was only a shame there weren't two of him, or four, or eight, to take me in every way possible again and again.

Bound in Blue
Monica Belle

BLACK LACE

Black Lace books contain sexual fantasies.
In real life, always practise safe sex.

First published in 2006 by
Black Lace
Thames Wharf Studios
Rainville Road
London W6 9HA

Design by Smith & Gilmour, London

ISBN 978-0-352-34012-2

Penguin Random House is committed to a sustainable future for
our business, our readers and our planet. This book is made from
Forest Stewardship Council® certified paper.

Printed and bound in Great Britain by Clays Ltd, St Ives plc

1

Was he going to do it, or not?

He was, lifting up his blue and white striped shirt to reveal a torso of solid muscle, the bronzed skin filmed with a subtle patina of sweat. Naked above the waist, he looked powerful, primitive, intensely male and, as his rich, strong laughter carried up to my window, I felt my stomach flutter. I could just imagine him picking me up so easily, to carry me off in his great brawny arms and thoroughly indulge himself with me in the changing rooms to celebrate his team's victory.

Why just him? There are fifteen men in a rugby team.

Why just the one team? No doubt the losers would like a consolation prize.

Thirty men. Thirty big, muscular men, wet with sweat and running with adrenaline after their game. There would be no nonsense, no twee little courtesies or awkward questions, no insecurity. They would just take me, enjoy me, as I would enjoy them – all thirty of them.

Not that it's easy to just give myself, not at first. I'd be ready enough physically after watching them play, and watching them strip off their shirts afterwards, just as my favourite had done on the pitch below my window. Mentally I might need a little more preparation, just to feel secure. Maybe I'd need to be cajoled a little before it started. Maybe I'd need them to lock the door to the changing room, just to make it clear there was no escape. Maybe I'd need them to tie me up . . .

'Dr Jones?'

I managed to withdraw my tongue and put on my serious academic face just before the door came fully open, only to ruin the effect by banging my knee on the leg of the bench as I tried to swivel my chair around towards my computer instead of the window and the sportsfields outside. As Tiggy Blackmore walked in she gave me a look that seemed more condescending than sympathetic, and I was sure hid a trace of amusement.

Out of my thirty-two students she just had to be the one to catch me gawping out of the window at the men on the sportsfields – Miss Tiggy oh-so-beautiful-oh-so-popular-never-seems-to-do-any-work-and-is-still-going-to-get-a-first Blackmore. Her perfect ten figure, her perfect face, her perfect confidence, all made me feel hopelessly inadequate; to say nothing of her waist-length natural blonde hair and her ability to dress as if she'd just stepped off the catwalk. I mean, how many students wear Prada shoes?

Even in her first year she'd been one of the most confident students I'd ever known, and a year and a half of life at Keynes had given her a polished familiarity I simply wouldn't have tolerated in anybody else. As I sat rubbing desperately at my hurt knee and trying to maintain some vague vestige of authority she sauntered over to the window, looking down on the men below, not in awe and longing, but with an expression better suited to an agriculturalist running an eye over a selection of prime stock.

'Been watching the rugby?'

'Yes.'

My answer had been somewhat sheepish, but she

didn't seem to notice. I quickly pulled myself together, refreshing the figures for farmland biodiversity on my screen as she went on.

'We really need more strength at the back, but we'll still be hard to beat as long as Josh is captain.'

'Josh?'

'The tall guy with the floppy black hair and no shirt on.'

'You know him?'

'Sure. We were together for a few weeks in my first year.'

'You split up? I'm sorry.'

'No big deal. Too much rugby and not enough me. I dumped him.'

I gave what I hoped would look like an appreciative nod for her decision, but my feelings were very different. Here was the man I'd been making the object of a fantasy, and she'd not only been out with him, but ended the relationship because he wasn't paying her enough attention. I knew full well what I'd have been doing in her place and at her age – bringing the oranges out at half-time.

Not that I'd have been with him, not when I was a student. I might have admired him from afar, but I'd never have admitted to wanting him, not even to myself. No, I'd have preferred to be protesting against EU agricultural policy or petitioning for new SSSIs, both far more worthy pastimes than indulging in hot, sweaty sex with some Neanderthal rugby player but, of course, it was impossible not to feel that I'd missed out a little.

Tiggy had turned away from my window and sat herself down on my bench, as if she owned the place. Any other student, particularly a male student, and I'd have told them to get off, but not Tiggy. She put on a slight frown, expressing a mild dissatisfaction that immediately made me feel I'd done something wrong and to want to help her in whatever way was possible, but if her essay was going to be late again I was going to have to put my foot down.

'What can I do for you?' I asked her, gently.

'It's a bit awkward. I've got an accommodation problem. I was wondering if you might be able to help?'

'Have you been to the office? You can apply for a change of accommodation, but you need to be able to show good reason.'

'Yes, I've been, several times. They gave me an assessment form and told me the adjudication process takes a month, but that my case is unlikely to be accepted.'

'You're in the Gaitskill Building, aren't you?'

'Yes. That's the problem. I just can't hack it.'

'What's wrong with it?'

'Everything, really. I asked for a north light because I draw, and they've put me at the corner, and with the other half of the block and all those sycamores there's hardly enough light to see at all. I've got this girl Nina next door too. She complains about everything, and I do mean everything. I don't get on with the warden, either, and it's making it really hard to work.'

I paused before answering, trying to balance my instinctive need to be helpful against the fact that her problems were obviously trivial. At least, they seemed trivial to me. She seemed to breeze through life without conscious effort, so perhaps found minor difficulties harder to cope with, or maybe it was because she wouldn't put up with minor inconveniences that she seemed to breeze through life. I couldn't see the accommodation office being impressed either way, and it was certainly nothing to do with me, as I told her.

'I sympathise, Tiggy, but I really don't see that I could help, except to say that you don't need to worry about your work. You've been late a couple of times, but you obviously do your research and you're also insightful.'

She shrugged, for once less than one hundred per cent assured.

'Thanks. Dr Jones, but what I was really hoping to ask is whether you'd consider letting me lodge with you. I know Sally Goulding did last year and I would really appreciate it.'

'Sally was a postgraduate.'

'Oh ... does that make a difference? I'd be happy to pay the same rent. I'd sort out my own food, everything. You wouldn't know I was there.'

I would. An image had come unbidden into my mind, of myself sitting in my living room attempting to read *New Scientist* while the ceiling shook to the passionate love-making of Tiggy and a large muscular partner, for some reason to the accompaniment of Beethoven's fifth. It was absolutely and utterly out of the question.

'I suppose that's possible, er ...'

'Great, thanks! That is so kind of you!'

'Um ... yes. When would you want to move in?'

'The sooner the better, please. I've just got to get out of that place.'

'The room is empty, so whenever it's convenient, I suppose.'

'Brilliant! There's one other thing. Do you think you could come around and get my stuff about eight?'

'This evening?'

'Sure, if that's OK?'

I was supposed to be meeting Robert at seven, but even so I very nearly agreed.

'Eight's not convenient, unfortunately. I could manage tomorrow evening, or the weekend.'

'Tomorrow's great. See you then.'

She'd already jumped down from the bench and would have simply left if I hadn't managed to pull myself together enough to stop her. I seemed to have already let myself in for having her as a lodger, and the rent was certainly going to come in handy, but I really couldn't put up with the boyfriend and Beethoven scenario. I was going to have to be firm.

'One moment, Tiggy. If you're going to stay with me there are going to have to be some house rules.'

'Whatever you say, Dr Jones.'

I've always made a point of treating my students as adults and as equals who just happened to be at an earlier stage of their education than me. Most of them still call me Dr Jones instead of Hazel, Tiggy Blackmore included, but by and large I've managed to dispense with the barriers of traditional authority, which I feel makes me more effective as a tutor. Inevitably there are some who bring the attitudes they learned at school with them to university, and others who take advantage of the situation, like Tiggy. Normally I manage to set things right, but with her it was different.

There's an aura some people have, something that sets them apart. Call it charm, or charisma, or presence, but it goes beyond simply being friendly and good looking, and can only really be appreciated face to face. Some pop stars and actors have it, a very few politicians, sometimes despite being as ugly as sin and downright arrogant. It gets things done, and Tiggy had it in spades.

It had never occurred to me to object to her employing me as a taxi service, and I'd come close to altering my own plans just to suit her convenience. I even felt guilty about going out with Robert for the evening, even though I knew that rationally it was ridiculous. Not that Robert would have minded. He never does, always accepting my decisions with a saintly forbearance for which I really ought to be grateful.

I am, I suppose, but it's just that occasionally I'd like a man who didn't always accept my right to personal space, who wasn't so ready to defer to my opinions, who wasn't always so correct. On paper Robert was my perfect partner, but I wasn't in love with him and being together did nothing to dilute my vivid fantasies of virile, primitive men or being physically restrained for sex. Inevitably if I did try to form a relationship with such a man it wouldn't last five minutes, or at least not beyond the first time he objected to me visiting male friends. Impasse.

Edward Albee's *Who is Sylvia?* was being performed by a touring group at the university theatre, and I'd wanted to see it for a long time. The production was well rehearsed and well polished, also delivered in front of a minimal set and with no clever effects or changes, allowing the power of the piece to come through without any distractions. It left Robert earnestly examining whether, despite all evidence to the contrary, he was in fact a bigot.

'It's so easy to become complacent about these things, and I think Albee makes us see that, and also teaches us that we must learn to extend our tolerance beyond those areas where it is little more than the safe option. Not that I mean to undervalue the importance of tolerance towards ethnicity, or sexuality, but those are, I think, instinctive, while in this case we need to examine what remains to many a deeply seated taboo.'

'Instinctive? I disagree. Human instinct is to distrust

what's different, and it takes a conscious effort to do otherwise. Tolerance is something we learn is right at a rational level.'

'You're right, absolutely, and it's an effort we all have to make. It's just that I now feel maybe I've been complacent about my own tolerance. Really I should be constantly reappraising my own attitudes.'

'Nonsense, Robert. You're the most thoughtful, caring man I've ever met. Anyway, we should really be beyond the stage of simply tolerating ethnicity or sexuality, because that implies putting up with something we'd rather not accept. With ethnicity or sexuality there should never be any question of having to accept things, any more than you would need to accept the colour of somebody's hair. I don't think Albee's motif is directly comparable, because in the case of Sylvia there are very real issues of consent and cruelty.'

He thought for a while as we walked down the Yarmouth road, nodding every so often to show he was ingesting what I'd said before he replied.

'You're right, absolutely, so rather than sympathising with Martin's need for tolerance we should see him as attempting to manipulate the other characters by using what is effectively emotional blackmail. It's certainly thought provoking.'

'Very, and funny too. I think he manages to combine a serious message with humour very effectively. Black humour, it's true, but still humour.'

'You're right, absolutely . . .'

We had to get across the road, which meant making a dash for it with a bus coming one way and a lorry the other, so I didn't hear the rest of his answer. As I reached the far side I was smiling to myself, wondering whether if I suggested that Albee had in fact been attempting to promote goat worship in Middle America he would have told me I was right, absolutely.

It was over a mile back to my house, and it had begun to spot with rain. Immediately I was wishing I'd compromised my principles and used the car. Robert wouldn't have approved, although he probably would have agreed with whatever rationale I chose to come up with. I'd always made a point of keeping my car use to an absolute minimum, which certainly didn't include theatre trips into town, but as we stood watching the yellow-lit drizzle beyond the inadequate shelter of the bus stop it was hard not to think of putting personal comfort first for once.

By the time I got home I was feeling cold and slightly fragile. That was where Robert really came into his own, putting together a thick vegetable soup while I sat down and sipped a glass of white wine. I'd taken to picking up all my vegetables once at week at the new farmer's market, which meant fresh, local produce and most of it organic, or at least untreated. The soup was delicious, and along with the wine it left me with a warm glow inside, a little drunk and a little tired.

Robert was still full of energy, but had switched from examining his own conscience to ways of making other people examine theirs, specifically recalcitrant landowners who were attempting to get around the right to roam laws. I was in two minds on the subject, balancing ecological considerations against a human right which, while valid, was also selfish. Robert had no such qualms, happy to view anybody who tried to restrict public access as an evil feudalist throwback, and definitely not including them under his umbrella of tolerance.

'. . . so we have to make these people see that we're

not just some rabble who need to be put in our place; they need to see that we are the people, and huge majority. Mark you, it's still iniquitous. Did you know that among EU countries the UK has the second highest proportion of land in private hands after Spain? It's like living in the Middle Ages!'

'Oh, I don't know,' I replied, somewhat indifferent to the issue, 'at least they can't put us in the stocks.'

'They'd like to.'

'I'm sure they would, some of them. So, what's the program for this Sunday?'

'Chalkpit Wood, near Newmarket. The owner's argued that access should be denied because the quarry makes it dangerous and they don't want to accept liability, so the council agreed they could fence it off, and even awarded them a grant. And do you know what they've done?'

I swirled the wine around in the glass, watching the light bounce off the rim.

'No.'

'Fenced off the entire wood, including an established right of way!'

'And what are you going to do?'

'Cut the fence across the footpath at the least. Some of us want to remove it completely, but I think we should minimise physical confrontation. Will you be coming?'

I hesitated, trying to find the courage of my convictions. He was right, and somebody had to make a stand, but I'd been feeling more and more that I'd done my bit after twenty years as an activist for more causes than I could remember, from my first outing with the local hunt saboteurs at fifteen. Yet too many people were making excuses, and apathy was as bad as defeat.

I nodded my agreement, provoking a pleased smile from Robert.

He glanced at his watch and swallowed the rest of his glass of wine before speaking. I knew more or less exactly what he was going to say.

'I've a nine o'clock tomorrow, first year Social Philosophy, but it would be great to make love, if . . .'

The question was left unfinished, allowing me to fill in all the criteria under which he was hoping I would allow him to invade my personal space. I'd have preferred him to pick me up over his shoulder, carry me upstairs and take me on the bed without even bothering to undress. It would never happen, not with Robert.

No. If I told him, he would do it; just as he did everything he possibly could to please me. He would do it, but it wouldn't be right. It wouldn't be real. He was caring, conscientious, faithful – everything he should be – which made me feel bad about wanting something else, so I smiled and held out my hand.

He took it, pulling gently to help me lift myself from the chair and holding on as we climbed the stairs, me with my wine glass still in my hand. At the door to my bedroom he kissed me and I began to respond immediately, my body reacting to his familiar embrace. As always, I would have to lead, the only way to overcome his exaggerated care for my feelings and the sanctity of my body.

Holding him close against me I moved carefully back to the bed and sat down, easing him gently lower by his shoulders. He took the hint, favouring me with a sly grin as he got down on his knees. A brief adjustment of my clothes and I was open to him, all the tension of the day beginning to drain away as he went to work. As I closed my eyes in bliss I reminded myself that it was another good thing about Robert: he was prepared to go down, and stay down, without stopping or complaining, until I had what I needed, and wouldn't even demand the equivalent favour in return.

I could take my time, and if there was a little guilt for what would be going through my mind while he gave me my pleasure, then I could console myself that he need not know, and could fondly imagine that my ecstasy came solely from the well-practised ministrations of his tongue. It wouldn't be true, because I had always needed to hold my pleasure in my mind rather than rely on my body alone, and this time would be no exception.

Something he'd said earlier had caught my imagination, something deliciously improper, something he and all my friends would be deeply shocked by if they knew it appealed to me, even as an impossible fantasy. It was how he'd said that some of the landowners would like to put protestors in the stocks if only they'd been able. I could just imagine it happening to me, not in reality, but as a fantasy – a fantasy in which there were no consequences, in which everybody got what they wanted.

I'd be caught cutting the fence. No, Robert and I would be caught, because it was only fair to include him. It would be the landowner, an arrogant young man, completely confident in himself, along with half-a-dozen burly farm hands, not one of them under six foot or two hundred pounds of muscle and bone.

There would be no argument, no choice. They'd simply tie my hands behind my back with bailing twine and frog-march me down to the local village green, Robert too. In the middle, where everyone could see, would be the old stocks, the sort where the person being punished has to bend down with their head and hands trapped. They'd put me in them, but only after they'd pulled my clothes off, every single stitch.

Robert would be watching, tied and helpless as I would be relieved of my clothes and fixed into place, completely vulnerable to all seven men. The young landowner would be the first, taking his right as the local squire to enjoy me as he pleased, indulging himself with me in every way before giving me to his men. There would be seven men, seven big, powerful men, taking turns with me, one at a time, two at a time, three at a time, over and over again as I reached climax after climax, which was exactly what was going to happen in reality.

I took hold of Robert's hair as it hit me, gripping hard and gasping out my passion as my body went tight with ecstasy. He stayed as he was, licking firmly until I could bear it no more and pulled him away. He rose immediately, eager for me yet still waiting for my nod of acceptance before allowing his body to settle on top of mine and sliding himself deep inside.

Tiggy Blackmore moved in to my house the following evening. I'd had visions of myself humping suitcases and trunks and bags and crates stuffed full of her belongings while she supervised me but, as it turned out, she had everything well in hand. When I turned up at Gaitskill House it was to find everything she owned being stacked on the pavement by no less than five young men: four rather alarming youths in black leather with their motorbikes parked on the pavement and a blond Adonis in a football jersey who carried a faint tang of fresh sweat.

The blond boy I took to be her boyfriend, but she treated them all in exactly the same way, always friendly, always laughing, and somehow managing to convey the impression that if they all behaved themselves and did their best to please her, she just might favour them a little, yet without ever in any way seeming easy. Rather, it was as if a smile from her was all the reward they could ever want, or even aspire to.

I watched her work her magic for a couple of minutes before getting out of my car. She hadn't realised it was me driving the little red Honda, but once I began walking towards her she recognised me immediately, waving happily before her expression changed to a slight frown.

'Oh. We may need to make two trips. Never mind, the boys can look after my stuff. Boys, this is my tutor, Dr Jones . . .'

'Call me Hazel, please.'

'. . . who's very kindly letting me have a room. Three of you better come with us, and the other two can stay here.'

She didn't introduce them, no doubt regarding them as mere muscle, but quickly had them organised so that once half of her things were piled into my car we drove across town with a motorbike escort. Tiggy chatted happily, taking her ability to corral large numbers of young men for granted but at least genuinely grateful for my help.

'It's so good of you,' she went on. 'I really don't think I could have put up with another night in that place.'

'Most people seem to manage.'

'I don't know how. It's like living in a rabbit hutch.'

'You were at private school, weren't you? Wasn't that much the same?'

'Sort of, I suppose, only I was with all my friends, girls I'd known for five years. I hated school anyway. So stifling.'

'You're school was single sex?'

'Saint Monica's Catholic School for Girls, near Arundel.'

'I had no idea you were Catholic.'

'Not me, not after having it rammed down my throat day in and day out all my life. It's all bollocks anyway . . . oops, pardon me.'

'Don't worry about it. What makes you say that?'

'You only have to look at the penguins. They think they're so perfect, but it's like all the blood's been drained out of them, like they're not alive. I know that sounds disrespectful, but it's true.'

'I'd have imagined you having rather a good relationship with your teachers?'

'Not at St Monica's. It was either their way, or no way. When I began to have doubts about my faith I tried to discuss it, but all I ever got was "I'm right, you're wrong". It just pushed me further away.'

'I can appreciate that.'

'And doing sciences I could see that a lot of what they were saying just didn't make sense. How am I supposed to respect somebody who says one thing in chapel and something completely contradictory in class? It's like doublethink, and we had the rest too. We used to call Mother Alicia's study Room 101.'

I had to laugh at the comparison, and just managed to stop for a red light, leaving my fingers tingling on the steering wheel. Tiggy didn't seem to notice, and as people and cars began to cross in front of me I went on.

'I don't think you can really compare a religious institution with Orwell's totalitarian regime?'

'No? It was about as just, I promise you.'

She trailed off, speaking again almost immediately.

'Do we have a choice with our project assignations?'

'I'll be putting up a list of titles, or you can choose

your own so long as you okay it with me or Dr Woolmer.'

'I was thinking of looking at the effect of tourism on biodiversity along the north coast.'

'That's possible, but if you want to look at biodiversity there's a chance to study a set of organic and non-organic farms, including those implementing the directives on beetle banks and field margins.'

'That would be good, but I was thinking of dune ecosystems, even trying to see how a decline in species numbers reduces stability.'

'You don't know that it does. Remember, gather your data first, draw your conclusions last.'

'Isn't it sure to?'

'You might think so, but that's just speculation. You must always start with a clear mind, even when you're trying to achieve an obviously worthwhile goal. Let's say, for example, that there was a proposal to build a new golf course along a section of remote dune land and you needed to make a presentation against it to the county council. Simply saying that you think there's a risk of destabilising the dunes and therefore of flooding isn't going to make much of an impression on the people making the decision, who you can be sure will be thinking of finances and votes ahead of the environment. You need to present solid data pointing towards a significant risk, preferably a risk to human interest so that it will affect them.'

'And if my conclusions are that there is no risk?'

'Then you have an ethical dilemma, but if you present weak data you're just going to end up looking foolish and, remember, business interests can always hire scientists to look at your figures, so they'd better be good. Getting back to your project, yes, it's a good idea but it will take a lot of work and may not produce clear results at all. Don't let me put you off though. It's a difficult project, but that will be taken into account for your final mark.'

She nodded thoughtfully and I returned to concentrating on my driving as we moved away from the lights. The centre of town was busy, but after a frustrating few minutes I was clear and decided to bring up my main concern about her lodging with me.

'I mentioned house rules, and I think we should have them clear from the outset.'

'I'm happy with whatever you decide on,' Tiggy said casually. 'It's your house.'

'It is, and I'm glad you see it that way. The first thing is guests. I don't want to seem fussy, and your friends are always very welcome, but I need you to use your discretion when it comes to those you've only recently met, particularly non-students, and I don't feel comfortable with the idea of men staying overnight.'

'That's fine. Let's just say nobody at all unless I talk to you first, and that way there won't be any problems.'

'I don't think it needs to be that formal.'

'Really, I prefer it that way.'

'As long as you're sure, but I don't want you to feel that I'm placing unfair restrictions on you?'

'You're not. I'm fine with that, really.'

It wasn't what I'd expected, just the opposite, in fact, but she was always so outspoken that it was hard to imagine her saying it just to please me. I felt immediate relief, now sure that the arrangement would work, yet coupled with a mild but irritating sense of disappointment. There would be no lying in bed listening to her making love, and nothing to spark the vivid fantasies that were becoming an ever more important part of my private world.

2

To my surprise, Tiggy proved to be as good a lodger as I could have hoped for. However much she disliked her upbringing and sought to reject Catholic values, it was evident that a great many of them had stuck. She was unfailingly polite and considerate, although absolutely sure in her own convictions, many of which were socially and environmentally naïve. Distinctions of class, background or wealth meant very little to her, presumably because everybody was tripping over themselves to be nice to her, especially men.

She kept her bargain, handling what seemed to be a never ending string of suitors with a wonderful combination of the firm and the flirtatious by mobile phone, and never once allowing any to set foot inside my house. Over the first weekend alone no less than six separate men called for her, in each case waiting respectfully at the bottom of the road until she chose to come out to them.

Five were just what I'd learnt to expect – not that I was watching or anything – young men with obvious appeal: a tall boy with a sensitive face and floppy brown hair; three sporty sorts including the blond boy who'd helped her move in, and also the most striking of her motorbike friends, with whom she went off for the Saturday afternoon. He struck me as the most attractive, lean and dark with an enticing hint of danger about him that I couldn't help but find arousing despite my best efforts to tell myself I was being immature.

The sixth man was altogether different, completely out of place alongside the others; he was older, pale, somewhat overweight and managing to convey an air of sweaty nervousness even at a distance of two hundred yards, fidgeting and hopping from foot to foot as they talked. It was easy to see that he might worship her, but impossible to imagine the feelings being in any way returned. After all, she had men at her beck and call, some of who might have stood in for anyone from James Dean to Hayden Christensen and no questions asked, while he was about as sexy as a boiled squash. Yet she kissed his cheek before he left.

Despite her faultless behaviour, by the time she came in on the Saturday evening I was feeling less than wonderful. I was already in bed, reading Flann O'Brien's *At Swim Two Birds*, which never fails to bring a smile to my face, but vaguely thinking I ought to put it aside in favour of *Historical Application of Nitrogenous Fertilisers and Ecosystem Decline in the Norfolk Broads*, while there was a nagging sense of dissatisfaction at the back of my mind.

I heard the motorbike from a long way off, a gravely roar rising from the background traffic noise and cut off abruptly at the bottom of the Close. Sure it would be Tiggy, I tried to resist the urge to peep out of the window for all of three seconds before pushing my covers back and swinging my legs out of bed. I hesitated, knowing that with my bedside light on I would be lit from behind and probably visible through the curtains before dashing through to the bathroom, which was dark. By standing on the stool I could see out from the open upper pane of the window, feeling foolish, guilty and excited all at once as I peered out.

Both Tiggy and her boyfriend were clearly visible in the pool of yellowish pink light cast by the streetlight on the corner of the Close. He had propped his motor-bike on its stand and was sitting on it, his helmet under his arm, looking up at Tiggy who had her own helmet dangled from one hand, the other hand on her hip and her long blonde hair hanging loose down the back of her leather jacket. It was a scene straight off a movie poster, impossibly glamorous, at least for me, yet for her evidently the most natural thing in the world. She kissed him goodnight, nothing more, but presumably because everything 'more' had already happened, leaving me feeling guiltier than ever for watching and with a dull ache in my stomach.

Common sense told me to go back to my book and attempt to overcome my despondency with a dose of Gaelic humour rather than pretend I'd been up and see if I couldn't draw Tiggy out a little about the events of the evening over a mug of something. What I really wanted to do – bring myself to a lingering climax as I imagined what might have happened between them – was going to leave me full of hurt pride and more despondent than before. I put on a robe and went downstairs, telling myself I'd let her talk if she wanted to but would not play the old mother hen.

I was just reaching for the tin of chocolate flakes when she came in, closing the door carefully behind her and putting the catch on as I called out.

'Tiggy? Would you like a mug of hot chocolate?'

'Yes, please.'

Her answer was completely casual, as if she'd been out to see a film with friends or attended a meeting rather than what I was sure she'd been up to, and with such a man. I took two mugs from the tree, measuring a heaped spoonful of the chocolate into each as she entered the kitchen, now with her jacket off to show the top she had on beneath. It was a T-shirt emblazoned with the name 'Night Owls', presumably a rock band, and the front was printed with the image of a huge and aggressive owl, positioned in such a way that the swell of her breasts made the eyes seem to bulge.

'Been to a concert?' I asked.

'No, just riding, up near Brancaster.'

I could imagine it, miles of empty dunes cut off by salt marshes, lonely, romantic, the perfect setting for her and him; walking hand in hand with the breeze in their hair, embracing at some sheltered spot, making love on the sunlit sand. It was years since I'd done anything of the sort, or at least the romantic part of it. My last walk with a man along a lonely shoreline had ended with Robert and me getting into an argument with a lobster fisherman who'd been taking undersized animals and females carrying their eggs.

She didn't elaborate, but sat down at the table as I made the chocolate. Again I had to remind myself that it would be intrusive of me to ask any direct questions, not to mention embarrassing for her. When she did speak it had nothing to do with her day, and again suggested that whatever she had been up to it carried little or no emotional weight for her.

'Do you mind talking shop, Dr Jones . . .? Hazel?'

'Not at all.'

'Good, only I ask in case you prefer to keep work and leisure separate?'

'No, in fact I've never really thought of it that way. What did you want to ask?'

'It took nearly an hour to get back from the coast, and Saul doesn't drive slowly, so if I'm to do my assignment on dune ecosystems I'm sure to miss quite a few lectures. Is that OK?'

'It's entirely up to you. You're not obliged to attend a single lecture if you don't want to, just as long as you know your subject. With your record so far I don't think you'd do any great harm, but make sure you don't give too much weight to the assignment.'

'OK, thanks. I may even stay overnight once or twice.'

'Again, it's entirely up to you.'

I could imagine who she would be spending the night with, and didn't even consider telling her to be cautious. It was hard to picture Tiggy as a victim, in any sense. Instead I let my interest in her project take over, and was still discussing xerophytes long after we had finished our chocolate, ensuring that I could drift off to sleep untroubled by disturbing visions.

Sunday was earmarked for our trip to Chalkpit Wood. Robert collected me shortly after nine, leaving Tiggy still in the T-shirt she'd worn to bed and yawning as she talked into her mobile phone to one or another of her men. With eight people coming, Robert had booked out the departmental minibus, while we were split over what action we should take, with me and Eve West attempting to mediate between the more extreme views. Sarah Innes, as usual, was for uncompromising direct action.

'There is no alternative. If they're going to behave like that we have to fight them with their own weapons.'

She illustrated her point by lifting the pair of bolt cutters she'd brought along, huge things more suitable for padlocks than barbed wire, which drew looks of horror from our pacifists, especially Marcus Shaw, who'd been shaking his head earnestly from the moment she started speaking.

'Sarah, please. We must not bring ourselves down to their level. What we must do is go to the farmhouse and present our case to them, outlining the legal situation –'

Paul Snell cut him off.

'They're aware of the legal situation, Marcus, and they don't care. They think they're above the law, these people. They think we're still living in a feudal society!'

He'd hit on Robert's favourite hobbyhorse, with inevitable results.

'Exactly, Marcus, they feel that their rights override those of the general populace. Justice, to them, is what they dish out, not what they take, which is why Sarah is right, although I do think we need to be more subtle about our actions.'

Sarah disagreed.

'No, Robert. To conceal our acts suggests furtiveness. Let's not have any doubt here. We're in the right. They're in the wrong.'

'We must at least speak to them first and inform them of our intentions.'

'Oh right, and lay ourselves open to charges of trespass and criminal damage?'

'Yes, exactly that! How better to bring the matter to the public attention!'

'We must avoid confrontation, Sarah!'

'No, we mustn't!'

'Yes, we must!'

'No.'

I stopped listening, turning to look out over the green Norfolk countryside. In my imagination I was back in the stocks, with a strapping young country Squire giving me a stiff talking to, then something else even stiffer.

They were still arguing when we reached Chalkpit Wood. I hadn't been there before, and was immediately drawn in by the quiet beauty, with a path running away from the road between hedges of blackthorn and chalk fields to either side. A group of hares was visible in the distance along one field margin, but quickly took alarm at our presence, running into the wood itself. This was set against the rising down, a cluster of great trees, mainly beech, cut into a broad crescent shape by the pit itself. A section of cliff was visible, the white earth mellowed by time, unlike the offending fence, which shone silver and the raw yellow of young wood in the sun, brutally new even at a distance. Sarah had given up arguing.

'I'm going to cut it. Anyone with the guts can come with me.'

She strode off down the path, closely followed by Paul. Robert threw me a questioning glance, but I'd already made my decision. It had to be done, and it was best done quickly and with a minimum of fuss. I followed Paul, and Robert followed me, then Eve, leaving the others standing by the minibus looking unhappy. Sarah was well ahead, and I had to hurry to keep up, with a bubble of tension growing rapidly inside me as we approached the wood, and bursting as I saw the fence, which had already been opened.

Fantasy is very different to reality. As we stood examining the cut fence and reading the notice somebody from the county council had nailed to a tree beside it, the owner of the wood himself approached us. He was everything I might have imagined, tall, arrogant, with a harsh, aristocratic face and absolute faith in being right, yet I had no wish whatsoever to have sex with him, while in the stocks or otherwise.

If he was self-confident to the point of arrogance, then he'd met his match in Sarah Innes, who could hardly have denied what she had intended to do while carrying her mammoth pair of wire cutters and would probably have confronted him anyway. I had little choice but to join in, leaving me with a bad taste in my mouth despite what we all did our best to see as a victory.

By the time we got back I was too tired to want to go out for a meal and had them drop me off at home. Tiggy was at the corner, talking to yet another admirer, who had just dropped her off. She was also tired, but otherwise in high spirits, and it was impossible for me not to compare our days: mine worthy but ultimately futile; hers devoted purely to her own pleasure and yet leaving her with a glow of well-being I was sadly lacking.

The day had also left me in a self-critical mood, not over our actions, but my response to the landowner. Was it wrong for me to fantasise over something that would have been so completely abhorrent in reality? Was even to allow such thoughts into my head a betrayal of all the values I'd held for so long? Or was it perfectly healthy and entirely harmless to have a vivid fantasy life and to react in whatever way my imagination suggested?

I was also unable to avoid making comparisons between my relationship with Robert and what Tiggy got up to. I told myself that there was nothing wrong, that it had simply become comfortable, predictable. If we agreed on most things and had many shared interests, then I should count myself lucky. Yet she made me feel that I was being too safe, that my life was dull and that with a bit of courage I could achieve so much more. I went to bed telling myself I'd had made all the right choices and feeling that I'd made all the wrong ones.

Unfortunately I couldn't get to sleep, my head too

full of contradictory thoughts and my body still full of adrenaline after our confrontation with the landowner. I knew I was going to have to do it eventually, or I wouldn't get enough sleep and I'd be in a bad temper the next day. As I rolled onto my back and let my thighs come wide I knew I was making excuses, but also that it was what I truly wanted.

A brief adjustment of bedclothes, nightie and knickers and I was ready, my eyes closed and my fingers busy as I let my imagination drift. It couldn't be Tiggy's never ending queue of admirers, because that would leave me feeling small. Even my favourite of being made a trophy for a group of sportsmen felt a little tainted, as she seemed to have been out with every worthwhile man both in university and town. The same applied for imagining my ideal man, as he would just end up turning into one of Tiggy's boyfriends at the crucial moment. A protest fantasy was better, but not the landowner and the stocks, because the reality of our confrontation was still too raw in my memory. The police were always a good standby, but the military better still, perhaps the US Airforce, which provided me with the perfect excuse for imagining myself completely helpless.

It would at one of the big air bases on the fens, maybe a protest against yet more land being turned into concrete and mown grass. Before they could bring the bulldozers in they would have to take down their own fence, miles of it. We would have chained ourselves to it, making it impossible for them to work, and my position would be the loneliest of all, a corner of fence pushing out into woodland, invisible from the base and screened by trees.

A group of military policemen would find me, four of them ... no, six, or even eight, under a sergeant, all young, powerful men, not one of them under six feet. They'd have no cutters and I would be totally helpless, my wrists chained to the fence, my body vulnerable to them in every way. Somehow they'd know what it was I really wanted, from my body language, from a few carefully chosen hints, but they'd know, and be sure that they would get away with it.

First they'd strip me, pulling my top and bra up high to leave my breasts bare, touching me as they pleased before pulling down my trousers and knickers, down and off, along with my boots, to leave me naked from the neck down. I would be shaking with need, unashamedly eager, to their delight and amusement. They wouldn't be shy, either, their cocks quickly out of their uniform trousers, already hard.

The only way they could take me would be from behind, so that was how it would happen, no choice, my bottom pushed out as they took turns with me, one at a time, the others watching and clapping, their erections ready in their hands, perhaps even in each other's hands. The Sergeant would be first, a huge man, six foot six and solid muscle, holding me steady as he eased himself deep inside.

His men would have to play cards for me, or roll dice, each winning the right to enjoy me, irrespective of my wishes. One after another I'd have to accept them, chained and helpless but so, so ready. Cock after cock would be pushed inside me, each taking his time and enjoying my body until he was satisfied, only to be replaced immediately by one of his fellow offi-cers. By the time the seventh was done I would be wriggling in ecstasy and begging to be allowed to come, so high I no longer cared for anything but pleasure.

The last man would take pity on me, a black soldier,

the tallest and youngest of them and so big it would seem that his beautiful cock was filling my whole body. He'd do just as the others had done, taking full advantage of my chained and helpless state before entering me, only instead of pawing my breasts or groping at my bottom he would reach around, tucking his hand between my thighs, exactly as my own hand was in reality, to bring me to climax, and again as he pumped into me, and again as he came himself, deep, deep inside.

Only then would I tell them the key to my chains was in my trouser pocket.

Monday was a great deal easier, with plenty to do and no procession of splendid young men other than those on the sports fields outside my window. Aside from lectures and tutorials my priority was to decide on the list of assignments we would be offering to our second year students. That meant an hour-long meeting with Dennis Woolmer and trying to keep the focus at least partially on environmental biology in the field and choices our students might reasonably be expected to complete.

Tiggy's choice at least suited his agenda, with its stress on human impact on the environment, and he accepted it without question. He even pointed me towards a similar study by a graduate at Bristol, looking at much the same problem on the Cornish coast. Another student had asked if he could create a computer model to look at the possible use of wave and tidal energy in the Wash, which I accepted after a moment's hesitation. A suggestion for a study of changes in urban fox populations was simply too ambitious and I had to scrap it, but by teatime I had a working list to pin up on the board, with Tiggy's name already against her choice.

As the students coming out of their three o'clock lecture clustered around the notice board I caught her name and an envious remark being made about how she always seemed to be one step ahead of the game. It was true, and as I walked back towards the common room I was thinking of how I was now helping to develop her legend.

She hadn't been in the lecture, and she wasn't at home when I got in. There was a note on the kitchen table saying she'd gone up to Brancaster and wouldn't be back, which left me with an unexpected empty feeling in the pit of my stomach and a sense of disappointment. I wasn't sure if it was her company I was missing or the sense of excitement she brought to the house, maybe both, but the sensation grew more acute as I made myself a salad and ate it, along with a solitary glass of wine.

It was also bin night, and after eating I poked my head into Tiggy's room, wondering if she had anything to collect for the recycling. There was plenty: magazines everywhere from *Elle* and *Vogue* to one on motorbike maintenance, two wine bottles and four alcopop bottles, all empty, and several drink cans. There were also clothes everywhere, and an extraordinary number of shoes, many obviously expensive but strewn about any old how. I hesitated, not wanting to make an issue of the way she chose to live, but not too keen to have to sort it all out once she'd thrown the whole lot together in a rubbish sack. The presence of a half-finished burger decided the issue, and I began to collect things up, leaving the magazines in case she hadn't read them, but taking the obvious rubbish.

One of the wine bottles was standing on top of a big, turquoise book, and as I lifted it up I saw the gold letters picked out on the cover – Diary. I smiled to myself, remembering how I'd kept a diary myself when I was her age, or rather younger. Life had seemed so special then, every day bringing something fresh, something worth recording. Not that my life had been anything like as exciting as hers seemed to be, and as I went downstairs with the bottles and cans I was feeling more wistful then ever.

I remembered hearing somewhere that only generals and virgins write diaries, just one of those nonsense sayings you come across. It certainly wasn't true in Tiggy's case, but it had been in mine and I'm no general. There had been boys enough, among the society meetings and protest marches, the campaigns for this and that, the political crusades. I'd just never been able to give myself the way Tiggy did, and my own needs had always seemed so trivial besides the problems of the world.

Despite studying environmental science, Tiggy didn't seem to worry about the problems of the world. She would even make a joke of issues like global warming, saying that if it meant she was likely to get a better suntan she'd be all for it. Certainly I couldn't imagine her letting it get in the way of her sex life. Nothing got in the way of her sex life, or so it seemed, and once more I fell to wishing I had been more like her – could be more like her. The highlights of her diary wouldn't be managing to get five per cent of the vote in the local council elections, or preventing the opening of a new McDonald's. No, they'd be what she'd been up to with Saul and her motorbiking friends, or the beefy blond boy.

Not that I was going to read it. That was out of the

question, a terrible breach of trust, utterly unthinkable, but very, very tempting. No, I wasn't going to do it, definitely not. I would have a nice mug of Fair Trade coffee instead and put all such thoughts right out of my head – Tiggy, her diary, what she got up to, and whatever she'd chosen to write down. Right out of my head.

Knowing her, it would be a lot. No, it would be *the* lot, every juicy detail. Exactly what had she been up to with Saul? Was it what I'd imagined or something else, something naughtier still? It would be there, I was sure, but I couldn't possibly read it, even though I had the whole evening to myself and no chance of being disturbed.

A coffee was not going to do any good. Nor was a glass of wine, which could be guaranteed to make my already beleaguered conscience even more fragile. Two glasses and I'd probably be reading the diary. Three glasses and I'd be reading it with a hand down the front of my jeans. Four glasses and I'd be ringing Saul to ask if he and his friends would like to come around and share me over the kitchen table.

Maybe not, although it was a tempting thought. How many of them were there in all? Four at least, or maybe six or seven. She didn't even seem to especially favour Saul, always careful to distribute her golden smiles and friendly conversation evenly. Could she? All seven? No, not even Tiggy.

Yet just how far did they go? Was Saul special, or one of the others? Maybe he was. Maybe they'd watched? If they'd watched, maybe they'd joined in? Was she strong enough? Did she have the sheer nerve? Maybe she did, but one way or another, it would be in the diary.

I was not going to read it, and that was that. There

was more recycling to be done, plenty of paper I could collect, perhaps some cardboard too. I could dispose of the old telephone directory for one thing, and both the local papers. There had been quite a large cardboard box in Tiggy's room, probably empty.

It was empty. It was also right next to her desk, where the diary lay, very big and very blue and very tempting.

Just a glimpse.

Just enough to see.

Just enough to know.

Just enough to spark my imagination.

I picked it up. I put it down again. I opened it, just to check it was hers.

Nothing on the first page. I turned the second. A date, a day, at the beginning of the year, before she'd come back to Keynes. I wasn't going to know anybody in it anyway.

January 1st Sunday

I write this sitting in Damon's car. Damon is a lucky bastard because I have just given him the New Year bj of a lifetime, on condition that he returns the favour, which he is going to do right now!

I stopped. It was enough, just like her, so bold, doing just what she wanted and making the boys play ball. Damon I could picture, the bestlooking boy around, the one everybody wanted, the one the girls would do things for just to have a chance. He'd be used to it, self-confident, tough, a bit of user even. Only not with Tiggy, oh no, she gave him want he wanted and demanded the same in return.

The guilt was raging in my head, but it was too late.

I'd done it. I'd looked, and there was no going back. To look a little more might be to compound my offence, but the worst was already done. I turned the page.

January 2nd Monday

What a night! Three times! Three times, and the third one on the bonnet of his car! That was the best, to be naked outdoors, such a thrill, and to think somebody might have been watching, watching me, and watching Damon, on his knees with his cock in his hand while he licked. Oh so good!

I closed the book, and my eyes. A strong shiver ran through me, my guilt forgotten in the sheer power of the image her words had conjured up in my mind. Damon, strong and dark, his lean young body naked in the moonlight, kneeling between Tiggy's open thighs, her fingers tangled into his hair. She'd come, carelessly naked out of doors, enjoying her own body without the least inhibition and so bold she was even excited by the prospect of a hidden watcher.

Her lack of description didn't stop me making a picture of the scene. Damon's car would be far from new, but big and powerful, bought to reflect his ego and his love of speed, and black – a Ford Capri maybe, or a Mustang. He wouldn't even know about emission levels, much less care. They would be in some lonely parking place, but not that lonely, with men watching from the bushes, full of envy and arousal as she got out of the car, gloriously naked and laughing, to climb on the bonnet and open her thighs. She would beckon to Damon, and he would come. She would point to the ground at her feet and he would go down, kneeling to her. She would snap her fingers to show him what he had to do, and he would do it, taking her to ecstasy under his tongue as he and the watchers masturbated together in an act of worship for her beauty and her power as a woman.

I would have been doing it myself, and I wanted to, then and there in her room. Her sheer confidence was overwhelming, the way she could control a man, making him perform for her, as eager as a puppy, down on his knees with his cock in his hand as he licked her, willing to do anything she asked just to please her. Robert was willing, always obliging, but that was because he felt it was how he should behave. With Tiggy it was as if they were begging for scraps from her table. I shook myself, trying to clear the image from my head, but it was no good. My gaze had already gone to the next page.

January 3rd Tuesday

Out with Kiyoshi at the UCS to see the three-hour Kaiju Eiga marathon, which put me well in the mood for a bit of B&D. Back at his place I told him to tie my hands behind my back and make me suck him off.

That was all, but it was enough, too much. Did she never stop? Wild sex three days in a row, and what sex. To picture her making Damon lick her on the bonnet of his car was bad enough, but this was more than I could handle. Before I could think to stop myself I'd popped open the button of my jeans and pushed my hand down to massage myself through my knickers.

I had no idea what Kaiju Eiga was, but it sounded Japanese, and so did Kiyoshi. He would be slender, dark-haired, very cool and mysterious, the film some cult movie full of beautiful Japanese girls being captured by gangsters, something to inspire Tiggy's need to have her hands tied, tied behind her back while she was made to suck his cock, made to . . .

There was no question of who had been in charge. It had been her choice and something I'd fantasised over so, so many times, to be tied up for sex, tied up and told what to do, all the responsibility taken out of my hands once I'd made that initial decision. I'd fantasised about it, but Tiggy had done it.

As I closed my eyes I could picture every detail, and I was already too far gone to care whether the Japanese boy was her boyfriend and unobtainable for me, or anything else beyond the exquisite little thrills already running through my body. He would have been sat back in an armchair, calm and easy, pretending Tiggy was his captive as she knelt in front of him, her clothing dishevelled, her hands tied behind her back, her mouth moving up and down on his cock as he held her by her hair.

I so wished it had been me, tied up and made to kneel, tied up with my clothes pulled aside to leave me showing everything. Yes, that was it, not Tiggy but me tied up and made to take a beautiful Japanese boy in my mouth; tied up and made to suck his cock; tied up and made to suck his cock in front of her as a punishment for reading her diary. I cried out in ecstasy as that final detail came to me, my whole body tight in a long moment of supreme bliss as I held the picture. Kiyoshi in his chair with his cock extending up into my mouth as I knelt before him with my breasts and my bottom quite bare; Tiggy standing watching, her arms folded casually across her chest, her mouth set in a cool smile.

If I hadn't bitten my lip I think I'd have screamed

the house down, because my climax didn't come in one great rush, but in wave after wave, each stronger than the one before, until at last my knees gave way so that I finished off kneeling on the floor in just the same position I was imagining myself. Feelings of guilt and confusion surged in as soon as I began to come down, but even beneath my self-recrimination I could still feel the satisfaction of one of the most intense orgasms of my life.

3

I told myself I would never look at Tiggy's diary again, but I knew it was a lie. Just knowing it was there was a temptation beyond endurance, and she made no effort whatsoever to conceal it. The most I could do was avoid going into her room, but that was not always possible as, at the very least, I had to make sure her windows were locked in the mornings. For four days I managed to behave myself, even while she was away, and it was a great deal easier once she was back from Brancaster, but the urge was still there.

Had it not been for what she had done with the Japanese boy I think I might have been able to cope, but as it was I couldn't. It was just too close to my own fantasies, and she had done them in reality. If she'd been 'in the mood for a bit of B&D' once, why not again? She was so casual about it, far more casual than I could ever have been, and that surely implied it wasn't even out of the ordinary for her. Just to think about what other experiences she might have recorded made me weak at the knees and I had to make a conscious effort to keep my mind on professional matters all week.

Without work to distract me I don't know what I'd have done, while I knew the Friday evening would be too much for me unless I stayed away from the house. Tiggy was going down to London to spend the weekend with her parents and, unless she took the diary with her, I was going to end up reading it. My only hope was Robert, who wanted me to lend moral support at his hunt saboteurs' group. I wasn't technically a member any more, having decided that with a ban in place it would now fade with time, but others thought differently, including Sarah Innes. She was incensed by the local pack's refusal to give up and determined to escalate our campaign. Afterwards, Robert was sure to ask me if I wanted to come home with him. He always did.

The meeting was in the reading room of the library where Sarah worked. It was in full swing by the time I got there, with Robert looking defensive and Sarah in full flow.

'... no reason whatsoever why we should curtail our program, not now, and not until they finally stop.'

A murmur of agreement ran around the table, mixed in with a little dissent and even less acknowledgement of my arrival as I pulled up a chair beside Robert, who had steepled his fingers as he replied, always a sure sign that he was feeling uncomfortable.

'All I am saying is that changing circumstances demand changing tactics, and that our most productive angle of attack now is to monitor their activities without direct confrontation.'

'No. Our task is to put a stop to this barbarism once and for all! We need to act, Robert, not to talk. Do you think we'd have ever achieved anything if it wasn't for people who actually got out there and did something?'

'No, of course not, and I have been involved with this campaign since nineteen eighty-one, but ...'

'Then what is your issue now? Getting too old for it, are you?'

'As I've tried to explain, Sarah, it's a question of tactics.'

'It's a question of stopping foxes being killed!'

I could see Robert beginning to back down as his desperate need not to be seen as a stereotypical male started to overcome his rationality. It was time I stepped in.

'Robert has a point, Sarah. The situation has changed and so we need to adapt to that. The law used to be on their side, but now it's on ours and we should take advantage of that. They would like to break the law, and they don't even deny it, so monitoring –'

'Yes, but the law is still inadequate!'

'Please let me finish, Sarah. Monitoring will allow us to ensure that they don't break the law, or that if they do we can bring a prosecution, which with luck could put a stop to their activities completely. Surely that has to be our goal?'

She looked thoughtful for a moment before replying, slowly, but with rising enthusiasm.

'Yes, of course, but if they know we're there they'll hardly break the law, so yes, we must monitor them, only not openly. Our new aim must be to capture an illegal act on video and bring a prosecution that will put an end to it once and for all!'

As she finished speaking she made a harsh cutting motion with her hands. There was an immediate buzz of excitement from her supporters, and not a single voice raised in dispute, mine included, despite the fact that the idea of sneaking around the countryside attempting to take clandestine footage of huntsmen and their followers had set my stomach tight with apprehension. Not that I had to go, which put a smile back on my face as I replied.

'There we are, then, a mutually satisfactory solution.'

Robert raised a finger.

'I still think –'

Sarah cut him off, simultaneously adopting the idea as her own.

'We'll vote. All in favour of my suggestion and putting the Breckland and Fen Hunt out of action for good raise their hands.'

Most of their hands went up immediately, the others quickly following suit when they saw they were out-numbered. I raised my own, member or not, and Sarah gave a nod of satisfaction.

'That's agreed then. How many camcorders can we get together?'

They began to plan the details, Sarah jabbing her finger onto the table as she made each point, setting out what each of them would do, as if planning a military campaign. I had to admire her, both for her commitment and complete lack of fear. Her strategy was to go in couples, each supporting the other, to ensure that whatever happened we got safely away with the all-important film. I knew from experience that most of us, probably including me had I been going, would play it safe on the day, sticking together with other, less militant protestors and near police. Not Sarah, she would be in the thick of it, and if she couldn't persuade anybody to come with her she would go in alone.

I was very glad I wouldn't be there, and that she wouldn't be choosing me as her partner. She ran, even marathons occasionally, and was also ten years my junior. That would inevitably have meant that if it came to the crunch she would be the one who fled with the camcorder while I would be left to face the wrath of the huntsmen, the followers, the terrier men, rough young farm boys . . .

It was the most outrageous scenario, totally unacceptable, yet I spent just a moment wrestling with my conscience before I'd begun to daydream, their voices now a soft background drone. The overriding need would be to let Sarah get safely clear, a need for which I would be prepared to sacrifice anything. I would be surrounded by a dozen men, maybe two dozen, all pumped up to the tops of their heads with adrenaline and testosterone.

One would make a joke, some crude remark on my figure, and something in my body language would betray my involuntary sense of arousal. They'd start to taunt me, suggesting that I needed a real man and volunteering their services. I'd try to deny it, angrily, at least at first, my instinctive reaction. Yet I'd know Sarah needed time to get away, and that only if they were all focused on me could she hope to succeed.

I'd start to taunt them back, telling them that if they were real men they wouldn't talk, but act. Some would be doubtful, thinking I was trying to trap them in some way. Others, the more earthy among them, would be thinking with their cocks, one especially, a huge man, six foot six of raw, male power, animal power. He wouldn't care for social mores, or for consequences. He would simply pull out his cock, a monstrous thing the same rich brown as the earth from which he would seem to have sprung. He'd ask me to suck it . . . no, he'd tell me to suck it, and I would.

It would, quite simply, be too good to resist, his sheer virility overwhelming, and to the cheers and clapping of the others I would get down on my knees in the long wet grass and take him in my mouth. I would already be lost, willing to indulge each and every one of them, but they wouldn't know that. As the huge man came to erection in my mouth another would step towards me, grinning, in his hands a length of bailer twine. He'd take my arms, firmly but gently, crossing my wrists behind my back and lashing them together. A second piece would go around my ankles, hobbling me, so that I could no longer run if I wanted too.

After that there would be no choices, no having to make the decisions. They would simply enjoy me, one by one, until I had satisfied all twelve, or another twelve, or the entire hunt, every last one. Yes, that would be best, and after all, why should any of them be denied their pleasure? There would be some piece of farm machinery, just the right height to lay me across, perhaps a giant roller smeared with mud.

They'd carry me to it and lay me face down on the warm muddy surface. They'd tear open my blouse, strong, coarse fingers pushing between my buttons to rip it wide, my bra too, spilling out my breasts to the cool spring sunshine. They'd pull down my jeans and my knickers, all the way to my ankles, leaving me bare and vulnerable behind. They'd touch me as they pleased, teasing my nipples erect and smacking my bottom. They'd have me, one at each end, the biggest, the most virile first, but all the others too, every single last one.

Sarah's voice snapped me out of my daydream.

'Is everyone clear what they're doing? Hazel?'

'Yes, of course, that's fine.'

I had absolutely no idea what she was talking about, and immediately realised I shouldn't have spoken so quickly. It was clearly the end of the meeting anyway, and Robert looked pleased with himself, smiling happily as I joined him at the door and kissing me before we stepped outside.

'Thank you, Hazel. Sometimes a point like that has to be made by a woman.'

'You're happy with the idea then?'

'It's not quite what I'd imagined, but yes, I think it's a useful, proactive choice. I have some gnocchi and pesto with sun-dried tomatoes at home if you'd like me to say thank you properly?'

He had his 'I'd like to have sex please, Hazel' smile on, to which I responded, but before I could say anything Sarah had come out, locking the reading room door behind her even as she spoke.

'Hazel, I need to speak to you, alone.'

'Of course. Excuse me a moment, Robert.'

She took my arm, leaving Robert looking more than a little fed up, and I allowed myself to be steered outside into the car park. I could feel the tension in her even before she spoke, and she glanced nervously to either side before she began.

'I need a favour, Hazel. Something very important.'

'I'll help in any way I can, Sarah, of course.'

'It's nothing difficult, only that if anyone asks what you were doing tomorrow evening between nine and one in the morning I was with you, OK?'

'But you don't plan to be?'

'No.'

'You're asking me to give you an alibi, in fact?'

'Yes, if you want to put it that way, but nothing can go wrong as long as you keep cool.'

'Sarah, I –'

'You know I wouldn't ask if it wasn't important, Hazel.'

'No, it's not that ... OK, so it is that. You know I'm trying to avoid anything even remotely illegal.'

'But you're coming to help monitor the hunt?'

'I am? Er, right, yes, but that's only trespass. This is serious, isn't it? I know by the way you speak, Sarah, so ...'

'Hazel, I need your help here! You're the only person I can rely on'

'How about Paul?'

'He's with me, but he has a separate arrangement.'

'Can't you be part of that? And anyway, what are you doing?'

'It's best I don't say. So you'll do it then?'

'I didn't say anything of the sort! But yes, if I was going to do it, I'd need to know, Sarah. It's not reasonable to ask me to take a risk like that without knowing why.'

She gave an irritable sigh, then answered in a rush of words.

'They're farming mink farm at Grendon again.'

'Mink! But that's illegal.'

'Not if they're for research purposes, it's not. But my bet is they're finding a way around the ban to sell the fur.'

'Shouldn't you take it to the authorities?'

'Be serious, Hazel, that would take for ever, not to mention the cost. It's better to act.'

'Not with mink, Sarah, absolutely not! I thought I'd explained to you how much damage mink do!'

'They're only following their natural instincts.'

'Sarah, mink are already causing serious imbalances in local ecosystems.'

'A few more won't make any difference then, will they? I'm going to do this, Hazel, and I would have thought you of all people would have offered your support. This is the fur trade we're talking about!'

'Yes, and releasing mink into the environment is not the way to go about putting an end to it.'

'We have no choice. They'll be in production in a week. Please, Hazel, say you'll help.'

'I ... I can't anyway, there's a student lodging with me at the moment, Tiggy Blackmore.'

'Then we'll have to say I was with you somewhere else. We'll go and look at ... at badgers. Yes, that's perfect. We'll go out now, you can reset the time and date on your camcorder and include me on the film. It's perfect!'

'Unless you get caught, and anyway, I'm going back with Robert.'

'Oh, come on, Hazel, what's more important, Robert or animal rights?'

I hesitated before answering, all too aware of the moral dilemma she was steering me towards, but for once determined not to give in to the pressure.

'Rights of course, but it's not a black and white issue, not when it involves the release of mink. I would help, you know that, but not on this issue.'

'Hazel ...'

'I'm sorry, Sarah, but this time the answer is no. I respect your position, but I must also ask that you respect mine and I can't be party to an act that causes so much environmental damage.'

She would have gone on, but Robert was drifting towards us, his patience no doubt beginning to wear thin. Instead she stepped forward to give me a brief and unexpected hug, then turned away. Robert replaced her, throwing me a questioning glance as soon as Sarah was safely out of earshot.

'You look upset?'

'It's nothing.'

It wasn't. The conversation had left me feeling irritable, but not for any reason I could explain to him. I knew I'd done the right thing, but I felt cowardly for not supporting Sarah, and also that I was rejecting a friend when she needed me. Not only that, but I'd lied to her, because Tiggy wouldn't be there on the Saturday night. Robert would have been understanding, perhaps asking a solicitous question to find out if I was pre-menstrual, which would only have annoyed me all the more.

I didn't say anything, letting him talk instead, all the way back to his flat. He badly needed to restore his ego over the compromise on the hunt sabotage, and I tried to help by making supportive comments. By the time we got to his flat he was a good deal more cheerful, but I was still struggling to shake my black mood, even as we ate. Half a bottle of wine had made little difference, and when he came to stand behind me and put his hands on my shoulders my first reaction was to shrug him off. I didn't, telling myself I was being silly, and he began to press with his fingers, a sensation too soothing to resent.

'You're very tense.'

'A little, yes. I suppose things have been getting on top of me.'

'Would you like me to give you a massage?'

'Why not?'

He began to press a little more firmly, and to use his thumbs to push at the muscles at the base of my neck. I closed my eyes, trying to relax and telling myself I was lucky to have a man who would spend so much time attending to me. It was true. None of the muscular, testosterone-fuelled men of my imagination would be the least good for me, let alone suitable for a long-term relationship, and yet there was still that nagging feeling that Robert lacked what I needed.

Yet I could no more turn him away than I could have kicked a puppy, and for all the dissatisfaction in my mind my body was reacting to his fingers, slowly but surely, my tension draining away to be replaced by a warm, comfortable sensation. I knew what was coming, what had been such a thrill the first time he ever did it, using the massage as an excuse to get me slowly naked, first my blouse, and then my bra, until at last the pretence was abandoned as his hands moved to my breasts. Sure enough.

'Let me undo your buttons, Hazel. It's so much more effective on the bare skin.'

I merely nodded, my eyes still closed as his fingers moved to my blouse, slipping my buttons open one by one, all the way down to my tummy. The sensation of exposure was pleasant, at last triggering sexual feelings in me, and as he eased my blouse down off my shoulders my imagination had begun to run. It felt rather nice, with my arms trapped by my sides and the front of my blouse open, rather as if it had been done to restrain me and make a show of my chest at the same time.

A gentle pressure from Robert and I had leant forward, allowing him to get at more of my back, now using his fingertips to make slow, walking motions from the nape of my neck downwards, all the way to where my blouse was now taut across my skin. I did feel good, as it was so soothing, and I could feel myself starting to react properly, my need rising as I imagined my chest displayed for some strong, uncompromising male.

'May I undo your bra strap?'

Again I nodded, and as he fumbled open the catch the sudden sense of release made me sigh. My cups had fallen loose, the material tickling my nipples as he went back to massaging me, each firm yet gentle motion of his fingers making my breasts move. Soon he would touch them, when he knew I was properly aroused, and as he held me he would suggest going into the bedroom, where he would take me to ecstasy under his tongue before climbing on top for his own pleasure.

I wanted something different, something more exciting, and as his fingers reached around to pull up my bra and take my breasts in hand I had decided what. He began to stroke, and to kiss at my neck, bringing up my arousal until I wanted to open my legs and let him in, or somebody else: a man who had the courage to make me open my own blouse, or simply rip it wide, to show off my chest, to admire me without embarrassment or uncertainty, perhaps with Robert watching. That was good, very good.

'Shall we go to the bedroom, darling?'

'No. Do it here.'

'Here? But . . .'

'Just do it, Robert. Go down.'

He didn't answer, and obeyed, as I'd know he would. I pushed back my chair, making room for him on the floor, now urgent as the fantasy I'd created grew more vivid in my mind. Who the man was didn't matter, only that he was intensely masculine, a clear alpha male, so much so that Robert would recognise it. I would be the object of the man's desire, Robert the help, using his skill with his fingers and tongue to arouse me physically, but it would be the man who took pleasure in me.

I'd pushed my jeans and knickers to the floor, opening my thighs to let Robert in. My arms still felt trapped in my blouse, my breasts exposed and vulnerable, which was just as I wanted it. As Robert settled down to giving me pleasure my mind was already racing, thinking of how I would be in the same position, with Robert on his knees and busy with his tongue while I was made to take the man in my mouth.

That was just as it should be, a clear, natural hierarchy, with Robert at the bottom, fit only to serve me, and me in turn given over to the pleasure of the man. I would do everything, never thinking to question the man's right as he enjoyed me, making me suck him, putting me on my back on the table and holding my legs, having me kneel for him to take me from behind; all the things Robert felt were too undignified for me as a woman.

Robert would watch, still kneeling, his cock in his hand as I gave myself completely, in a way I'd never been able to with him. Yet there would be no jealousy. Robert would know where he belonged. Maybe he would even be called on to provide the pleasure of his mouth as the man and I made love, kissing my nipples as I rode the man's lean, hard body. Better still, behind me, to kiss and lick, his face just inches from the man's cock and balls. Best of all, serving completely and willingly, taking my man's balls in his mouth.

My body went tight, the picture hot in my mind of how it should be, with Robert given over to my pleasure and the man's as well, serving us both, because to a male so, so virile it made no difference if he was a boy or a girl, and he would know it. The man would lie down on the table, his beautiful erection rearing up from his body. I would climb on, taking him into myself as deep as I could, and look back, motioning to Robert.

He would respond, maybe with a little chagrin, but he would know a true alpha male when he saw one, and that by comparison all he was fit for was to give what pleasure he could. Down he'd go, his mouth wide, to take in the man's balls, sucking as I rode, my bottom slapping in his face, and tugging on his own cock as he did it.

I was coming, wave after wave of ecstasy sweeping through me, and Robert never so much as slowed down until, at last, I could take no more and pushed his head back. He came up immediately to take me in his arms and kiss my breasts, my face, my mouth, his cock hot and urgent against my leg. I let him go inside, urgent and clumsy, but too excited to need more than a few firm pushes before it was all over.

I had managed to keep both Tiggy and her diary out of my head all evening and all night; so that by the time I left Robert's on the Saturday morning I was wondering why I'd made such a fuss over it in the first place. Even when I got home it didn't seem particularly important, and I settled down to read through my students' essays, which proved to be the perfect antidote, at least at first.

Hoping to make them think rather than simply feed back what they'd picked up in lectures and from set texts, I'd created models of possible future climate change allowing for different levels of global warming. Most had simply looked up the existing models equating rising carbon dioxide levels with changes in temperature and illustrated this with predictions ranging from those already apparent, such as glacial retreat to the speculative, such as the breakdown of the Gulf Stream. Only Tiggy's stood out, with not only a much more critical look at the existing models but a detailed analysis of existing and predicted changes in species distribution, illustrated with records of increasing langouste catches in the English Channel.

I hadn't even seen the data myself, although it had presumably been published somewhere as she obviously hadn't had the time or the resources to gather it. It still showed remarkable enthusiasm, not to mention intelligence, especially as she never seemed to be stressed by work and led such an active social life. Aside from the abundant male attention, she was involved with several different sports, also various societies, so that just about every moment of her time was taken up.

That set me wondering. At the time I'd been too nervous and too aroused to think at all clearly, but there was something peculiar about her diary, or at least that part of it I'd seen. She had only recorded her sexual exploits, with just the occasional comment about her day-to-day life and those generally relevant to what she'd done with some boy or other. It seemed an odd way to go about things, unless it was specifically intended as a record of her sex life. Yet that seemed unlikely for a girl at once so popular with the men and so casual about her relationships.

I went back to my essays, reading through and marking, but the diary had got firmly back in my head. Before long I was telling myself that just a glance wouldn't hurt, if only to see whether her style changed after she'd come back to university. I tried to fight it, first turning the TV on, then attempting to immerse myself in Flann O'Brien. Neither worked, my curiosity growing despite myself.

Maybe, just maybe, I'd have succeeded, but when I finally went upstairs to bed I found her door open and her bedside lamp still on, with the diary on her desk, large and blue and tempting. I had to turn the light off anyway, but the guilty thrill of stepping into her room and remembering what I'd done before was just too much. My hand went to the diary and I had opened it, telling myself I would just glance at a few more pages from January to see if her entries became more detailed. They did, a little, but not in the way I'd expected.

January 12th Thursday

> *Back in the jug again, in a great room right next to Nina and Emmy. Went riding with Saul up to Grim's Heath and stripped off to go on the back! Felt so good I just had to have it then and there, on the saddle, no clothes on and anyone might have seen!*
>
> *Saw X in the evening. Feel the same as ever, maybe more.*

That was it, just a few lines, but fascinating and also disturbing. I shut the diary, having plenty to think about. First there was the apparent anomaly of her satisfaction with her room, yet she had had several weeks in which to change her mind. Far more intriguing was her comment about X, which was remarkably coy for a girl who was not only prepared to ride naked on the back of a man's motorbike, and have sex with him, but to revel in her exhibitionism and to record it with open pride.

As I went to my own room I was wondering if it was possible to identify X. Whoever he was, she had seen him on the evening of Thursday the twelfth of January, and it might just be possible to find out what she'd been doing at the time. Only then did my guilt overtake me, and I pushed the thought out of my head. To read her diary was bad enough, but to try and uncover what was obviously a very personal secret was far worse.

I had at least only taken a peep, a small dose, but sufficient. As I undressed and showered I was already thinking of how it would feel to ride naked on the back of Saul's motorbike, and I never even made it to bed, but had slid one soapy hand down between my thighs almost as soon as I'd stepped into the shower. A few touches was all it took, with the hot water cascading down over my body and the mild sting of the soap helping to bring me rapidly up towards my climax as I imagined Saul easing me forward across the tank of his motorbike and slipping into me from behind with Tiggy watching, also naked but cool and calm, her mouth turned up in her familiar smile.

4

I half expected the Sunday paper to carry a picture of Sarah and Paul being led away in handcuffs, but there wasn't so much as a mention of Grendon, mink or anything to do with animal rights activists at all. The front page was given over to some royal who'd managed to put his foot in his mouth, an event too trivial to be worth reading about. I had hoped there would be some mention, and while it was possible the news simply hadn't broken early enough to make the papers, I was left with a sense of anticlimax.

With my essays marked there was nothing that urgently needed doing, and after a morning of half-hearted chores I was once more beginning to think of the diary lying up in Tiggy's room. I nearly gave in, but my guilt got the better of me and I decided to go and see Sarah instead, curious and also keen to make up with her after refusing to help. By long-standing agreement we never discussed anything she did on the phone when there was a risk of prosecution, so I walked over. She was there, still in her robe, speaking immediately she saw it was me.

'We did it, Hazel.'

'You did?'

'Yes. You should have been there. I know you disapprove of releasing mink, and I respect that, but you should have been there.'

'Thanks, I appreciate that, and I've been feeling bad for letting you down. What happened?'

'Everything went to plan. They are bastards, these *people*, they really are. The whole place was set up just like it used to be before the ban, with mink in two long sheds, in tiny cages, the absolute minimum they can get away with under ninety-eight/fifty-eight. They were dead arrogant too, because all they had was a six-foot chainlink fence and a really basic alarm. We cut in at the back and Paul had the alarm down in under a minute. After that it was simple, although we had to physically remove some of the mink from their cages.'

I nodded. She was still brimming with excitement, just as I would have been if I'd come. Instead I'd spent the evening marking essays and playing with myself over Tiggy's exploits with her motorbike-riding boyfriend. For all my ambivalent feelings it was hard not to admire her. Like Tiggy, she preferred to act rather than to talk or think.

'You know my feelings, Sarah, but well done anyway.'

She smiled and hugged me.

'That's OK, Hazel. Like I said, I respect your position, and you've done plenty. Coffee?'

'Please, yes. So you didn't need the camcorder after all?'

'It might come in useful, you never know, although we were pretty careful. Talking of filming, how many people do you think will make a serious effort next Saturday?'

'I'd been wondering about that. About half?'

'If we're lucky. Eve will be OK with Paul, there's you and Robert, but that's about it. Is there anyone else you could recruit? Some of your students maybe?'

'I'm not sure. None of them are especially politically aware at the moment.'

'How about your lodger?'

'Tiggy? I doubt it. Her work's very good, but I think she's chosen environmental biology more for the sake of a career than from any interests in animal rights.'

'Ask around, anyway.'

'I will. Do you have anyone in mind?'

'No. It's getting harder since the ban. Everyone seems to think it's all over.'

'That's certainly true, and hopefully it will be in a year or two.'

She nodded, but without any great enthusiasm. Not for the first time I wondered how much of what she did was purely for the thrill. There was no question that she cared, and yet it was easy to picture her releasing ant farms back into the wild if there was nothing else to do.

I spent all day with Sarah, talking over the six years we'd known each other, since she'd been a student and the things we'd done together. By the time I'd left I was feeling more than a little nostalgic and thinking about life. Looking back, I'd been just as determined as her, if always rather more cautious. Just as Tiggy made me feel I'd missed out, so Sarah made me feel I was slowing down.

As I approached the corner of the Close I saw Tiggy herself, standing talking to Saul. The big rucksack she'd taken home was still on her back, so presumably he'd picked her up from the station, running to do her bidding for all his tough image. She waved as I approached, flashing her brilliant smile.

'Hi, Hazel. You've met Saul, haven't you?'

'Yes, of course, when you moved in.'

She obviously didn't even remember who'd helped her that day, but carried on blithely as Saul gave me an indifferent nod. I couldn't help but remember what she'd written, and what I'd thought about, bringing the colour to my cheeks as Tiggy told me about her weekend. If it showed then neither of them seemed to notice, and he was clearly waiting for me to go, no doubt in order to make some suggestion to her. She was indifferent, chatting happily and after a while she gave him a kiss clearly intended as a goodbye. He took the hint, mounting up and swinging his motorbike around in the road before roaring off into the distance. Tiggy took no notice whatsoever, still talking to me.

'... an interactive installation, so that you become part of the artwork yourself. That's amazing, and the sense of space and light too, so that when you come out everything seems more real, more intense. There was an exhibition of airbrush art too, in a sort of crypt under a church in Borough. Michael English and a few others, not stuff you see very often. How about you?'

Not only had she been to see her parents, but she had managed to take in two art galleries and go up in the London Eye, which was just the public bit. Suddenly admitting that I'd sat at home marking essays was out of the question, never mind thinking wistful thoughts largely centred on her sex life.

'This and that, mainly arranging things for next week with Robert's group of hunt saboteurs. We aim to take some footage that will close down the Breckland and Fen once and for all, with luck.'

'I really admire that, you know, standing up for what you believe in when you don't get anything out of it.'

'There's a great deal of personal satisfaction. You should come, we need new faces.'

'Me? I'd love to, only I don't think I could face having people shouting at me or anything like that.'

'No? You seem very capable to looking after yourself.'

'I hate that sort of thing, but I would like to be involved in some way.'

'Take your time to think about it, but you're very welcome.'

'Thanks.'

We'd reached the house and I let us in. Tiggy quickly went upstairs to dump her rucksack and I was left feeling grateful that the temptation to read her diary could be set aside at least for the time being. I'd had nothing to eat all day and had begun to search about for ingredients when Tiggy came back down.

'Have you eaten, or are you going out?'

'I'm not, no, but don't worry about me. Unless you'd let me treat you in someway, to say thank you.'

'That's very kind of you, but I really can't ask you to spend anything on me.'

'No, really, I don't mind. There's a new vegetarian restaurant in Well Street.'

'The Artichoke? I couldn't possibly expect you to take me there, Tiggy.'

'It's the least I can do after you've been so generous to me. I'm fine for money.'

I hesitated, thinking of the designer clothes she wore so casually. Her family was evidently well off, and presumably supported her, which put rather a different complexion on things.

'That would be very nice then, if you're sure?'

'Absolutely. I'll just get changed.'

She ran upstairs again and I followed, intending to splash a little water on my face and perhaps run a brush through my hair. Tiggy had disappeared into her room and was still there when I came back down, leaving me twiddling my thumbs as she used the bathroom in turn. When she did come down she'd not only changed completely, but into a beautifully tailored red gown with heels to match and her hair twisted up onto her head. She'd also made up and put on a subtle perfume I didn't recognise, so that she looked better suited to a formal ball than a restaurant. My surprise must have showed, as she coloured a little and looked down.

'It's not too much is it?'

'No, you look lovely.'

'It is, it's far too much. I should change.'

'Don't, please. You're fine, as long as you don't mind being seen with me.'

She laughed, a touch nervous, and I wondered if she might have some ulterior motive for wanting to go to The Artichoke with me, perhaps an admirer, although it was hard to imagine why she'd need company. I put the thought from my mind as we left the house, sure that, like me, she was simply a little nervous at being in a purely social situation with somebody who was usually in an unbalanced relationship, either tutor and student or landlady and lodger. If so it didn't seem to have affected her easy conversation, happily picking up from where she'd left off earlier.

'Today made me think about fashion and art. The installation in the Tate must have cost thousands of pounds, maybe tens of thousands, which at least implies it's something really important. It was good, and I suppose helped me to look at things more clearly, but the airbrush art held my interest for much longer. So what is it that puts one in one of the biggest and best known galleries in the country and the other in a crypt? Just fashion?'

'I suppose so, although I'm sure an expert would be able to explain, or at least to provide an explanation.'

'Which isn't the same thing, is it?'

'No. It's not my subject, but it seems to me that many modern artists feel that simply proclaiming 'I am an artist' is enough to make it true. I suppose the best known example is Tracey Emin.'

'She's the one who did the bed, and a tent with the names of all her lovers? I rather liked that.'

I'd thought it was awful, perhaps due to a touch of jealousy because my tent would have had precisely five names, but I didn't want to get into that. We'd reached my car, but I didn't even hesitate before walking past, not on principle, but because I wanted a glass of wine. I answered Tiggy's question as we turned towards town.

'Maybe, but is it art? As a scientist I find that rather hard to accept. Anybody could do it.'

'But they didn't.'

'That's not necessarily true. They might well have done, but they didn't proclaim it as art and have the necessary contacts to make other people take notice. It's the same with your two exhibitions. The Tate installation has the approval of the establishment, by definition, so it's easy to accept it as art. Maybe I should say it's safe to accept it as art.'

'How do you mean?'

'Again, this isn't my area, but it is Robert's.'

'Robert's a sociologist, isn't he?'

'Yes. He'd argue that the majority of individuals within any given social grouping will wish to be perceived as high status – high status according to the criteria by which the group judges status. Thus a male in a primitive, warlike society would wish to excel at feats of arms. Our modern society is no different, only more complex, and knowledge of certain fields is considered important. Art is one of those fields, but the definition of art has become fluid. It used to mean skill, and there wasn't a great deal of difference between art and craft. That's changed over the years, so that modern art is all about expression and doesn't necessarily require any skill at all. Because of that it's much harder for the general public to appreciate, and so critics are required to interpret pieces. Most people don't have either the time or the inclination to make an in-depth study of the subject, but still want the status associated with it, and therefore take up the positions put forward by the critics instead of establishing their own. Unfortunately it seems to me to mean that the famous artists are no longer the best, but simply the best self-publicists, or even the ones who happen to have slept with the right critics. So everyone's saying how marvellous the Tate installation is while the airbrush art languishes in a crypt, dismissed as shallow by the critics and therefore also by everyone except ardent enthusiasts and those with no preconceptions.'

'So which do you think is better?'

'I'm not even sure there's an answer to that. Art is inherently subjective, and so defies proper analysis. As a scientist I find it difficult to set too much store on something that relies on opinion rather than fact.'

'So you're saying that science is more important than art?'

'I'm saying that science is a more serious discipline than art, or at least it has become so. Let's say, for example, that the county council commissions a piece of art for a new shopping centre. If it's bad people will make a joke of it, but that's hardly important. The worst you can say is that it's a waste of public money, but the council could argue that it brings in shoppers and even tourists, but only if they receive publicity, which in turns means spending a lot of money on a big name. Maybe it makes sense, sometimes, but the irony is that the poorer the piece of art with respect to what's been paid for it the more publicity it will get!'

She laughed, which made me feel unexpectedly good and I went on.

'On the other hand, the council might commission a study from me, perhaps on something not dissimilar to your assignment, looking at the stability of sand dunes and whether tourism has a significant effect on erosion. Like the artist I am paid and the result is left to my judgement, but unlike the artist I need knowledge and skill to achieve my purpose, and not merely the good opinion of my peers. For the artist failure and success aren't even clear-cut concepts, but if I fail and the result is that a dune bank gives way during a storm then it could mean immense damage to the environment and to property, even loss of life. That's why I'm a scientist, but I don't know why I'm telling you this. To judge from the quality of your last essay you've obviously thought things through.'

Her response was a shrug and a smile, perhaps a touch embarrassed by my praise. We were close to a bus stop and one was approaching, so we boarded and rode the rest of the way into town, still chatting, although she quickly steered the subject away from her project, not wanting to talk shop. For all my efforts to treat my students as equals there was usually at least something of a barrier, but with Tiggy that was beginning to break down, and as we made our way to The Artichoke she was calling me Hazel and telling me how she'd got her nickname.

'Since I was at primary school I've had this name, because I used to be like Tigger, in Winnie the Pooh.'

'Yes, I can see that.'

'I liked it so much I'd tell people it was my name and refuse to give my real one.'

'Which is? If you don't mind . . .'

'Mary, but I never use it, ever.'

'I must admit it's hard to see you as a Mary.'

'Everyone says that, except my Mum, and the penguins at Saint Monica's. Half of them were called Mary too, which really put me off.'

'I'm sorry you had a bad experience at school, but it doesn't seem to have affected you.'

'Oh, I don't know. I've rejected it all, but it's hard to get rid of. Like sometimes I feel guilty about things when I know there's no reason to, just from years of having it drummed into me that I should.'

'I'm surprised. It certainly doesn't show.'

'It wouldn't, because I recognise it and make a point of going against it, but it's still there, deep down.'

I was very surprised at what she was saying, because she certainly hid it well, both in the way she behaved in general, and in private too, if what she'd put in her diary was anything to go by. As we took our menus it occurred to me that perhaps she focused on her sex life as a form of catharsis, taking a deliberate pride in what she did as a reaction against the moral strictures her Catholic education had tried to impose on her. It made sense, and left me more intrigued than ever, and guiltier, only my guilt was entirely justified.

'What do you recommend?'

She was studying the menu, her expression for once a little uncertain. Her usual diet seemed to consist of whatever she could grab in passing, which meant mostly fast food of the worst sort. I hadn't said anything, not wanting to interfere, but now seemed to have a chance to convert her.

'That's rather a matter of taste. You should try some-thing with tofu, perhaps with roasted onions and pep-pers and new potatoes in basil mayonnaise, which is what I'm going to have, or the Catalan tortillas with organic goat's cheese and pesto are sure to be good.'

'I'll have whatever you're having.'

She was still uncertain, and she stayed that way, enjoying some things, only doing her best to enjoy others. Even the way she held her cutlery suggested a slight lack of confidence, while as we worked our way down one bottle of wine and a second our conversation grew ever more open, so that for the first time I began to feel I was seeing through her poise to the young woman within. By the time we left she had really opened up to me, showing her age and even some degree of inexperience as she spoke about Saul and others.

'It's like a balancing act, all the time. I want to be friends, but it's so difficult with men, because they always seem to get jealous. Saul's great to be with, but he's already starting to get possessive, you know, ask-ing where I've been and showing off in front of his mates so that it looks like I'm his exclusively. I don't want to be seen as belonging to somebody.'

'Have you talked to him?'

'What can I say? Last time I tried that it ended up in a massive row and now we don't speak. That was with a guy called Damon, who I was seeing back at home. We used to have a great time, but when I suggested we didn't need to be faithful to each other while I was at uni he blew his top. We hadn't even talked about faithful before, he'd just assumed it. I'm sure Saul would be the same.'

I remembered Damon, the boy she'd made go down on her on the bonnet of his car. It was hard to know what to say, because I could understand his feelings more easily than hers. For any man to fall in love with Tiggy would have been all too easy, and with love comes jealousy, almost always. Before I could find some suitably noncommittal but supportive comment she went on.

'He's always trying to put Gareth down too, as if just because I like both of them there has to be this big rivalry thing going on.'

'Gareth is the blond boy you see sometimes?'

'Yes. He's sweet, but he's no different underneath.'

'I'm afraid that when you become intimate with men there's sure to be jealousy.'

'Why? I only want to be friends, and I don't go for this 'women are from Venus, men are from Mars' rubbish. If you think men get jealous you should have seen the girls at Saint Monica's, they were ten times worse!'

From what I'd read I knew that if her relationships with Damon and Saul were typical of what she considered friendly, then it was no surprise they got jealous. It would have been an extraordinary man who didn't, but I could hardly point that out.

'I'm afraid it's just an element of human nature, and as you're particularly attractive it's inevitable you'll often be the focus of men's jealousies, women's too, as a friend. Look on the bright side, at least they want you. Imagine how it would be if you weren't attractive.'

'Am I so attractive? I don't know.'

'Frankly, yes.'

It was true, of course, that she saw herself from the inside and not merely as a set of curves pleasing to the male eye, yet aesthetically surely there could be no doubt? She merely shrugged. I wanted to give her advice, but there was no easy solution.

'I'm afraid it's just something you'll have to learn to put up with, Tiggy. If you don't want to commit but do want to be honest, then you're always going to run into this sort of problem. Or if you don't mind being a little dishonest, just say you only want to be friends, but when the moment comes . . .'

I left it unsaid, suddenly sure that when it came to relationships she would be well ahead of me and that for all the differences in our ages she would be the grandmother in the egg-sucking discussion. No doubt she didn't want me to feel bad, because she turned to me with a big smile.

'Thanks, maybe that's it. I don't mind being a little dishonest.'

We didn't bother with the bus, but walked all the way back to my house, talking as we went on a dozen different subjects, both general and intimate, serious and trivial. It was gone eleven by the time we got in, and with a nine o'clock lecture to give I knew I should be making for bed. Tiggy had no such qualms.

'I've really enjoyed this evening. Shall we have another glass of wine, if you don't mind that is?'

'Better not, on a Sunday, but another time would be great. Just a chocolate, maybe. I've enjoyed myself too, and that was very generous of you. Thank you.'

'We must do it another time. Chocolate would be great.'

As I made the chocolate and we drank it together in the kitchen I could feel my tiredness stealing over me, physical tiredness anyway. My mind was still buzzing, full of different thoughts and emotions. When we went upstairs I said goodnight at her door, which was wide open, with her diary on her desk. She had presumably filled it in before coming out with me, or had left it out to remind herself, and it was impossible not to wonder what she would say.

I was still full of nerves as I undressed and washed. I had finished *At Swim Two Birds* and moved on to *The Poor Mouth*, but not even O'Brien's wit and the peculiar behaviour of Bonaparte O'Coonassa could help me to relax. Part of me wanted to masturbate very badly indeed, an instinctive response it was hard to accept rationally. My long evening with Tiggy had changed things, making it harder to see her as a fantasy substitute for myself, while what she had said about Saul made him less appealing as an idealised male. To imagine her watching as he made love to me no longer felt right, now too personal, yet I wanted to do it.

When I'd finally given up trying to read and turned the light out I lay staring into the darkness, one hand resting on my tummy as I wondered if I should or shouldn't, and whether I could resist the disturbing thoughts building up in my head. Tiggy was just next door, and it seemed very odd indeed to want to play with myself over some fantasy in which she was sure to be involved, only as a watcher admittedly, or at the very most somebody to tie my hands.

My resistance was slipping, all the wine I'd drunk making it hard to combat my darker feelings, as well as an extraordinary rush of adrenaline. Maybe I could allow myself a little leeway and just not think about Saul, or Gareth, or Damon, or Kiyoshi, or Josh, or any of the other men she'd mentioned during the evening. Unfortunately that left the pasty-faced one I'd seen her talking to the week before, who really was not my idea of a male fantasy figure. There was only one choice, pure imagination and my archetype male, last seen with me straddled across his hips as Robert sucked on his balls.

Just the thought sent a shiver through me so strong it was like a miniature orgasm. I gave in, closing my eyes and biting my lip as I slip my hand down the front of my knickers. With Tiggy involved the roles would be rather different. She would be the focus of his attention, leaving me to provide service with my mouth and hands, me to kneel in front of him and bring him to erection as she watched me kiss and lick at his balls as she rode him.

I remembered a word from an article condemning the US porn industry: fluffer – a woman whose sole task was to keep the male actors aroused in between scenes. At the time I'd been horrified, although even then the idea had spoken to something deep inside me. Now it seemed utterly compelling, only not for some sordid film, but simply because it was the right place for me in my fantasy, the only possible place. I would be their fluffer, stark naked, my job to keep him ready for her pleasure, taking him in my mouth again and again as they made love, my sole release my own fingers.

No, they'd want to keep my full attention, not have me worrying about my own pleasure when it was theirs which mattered. Tiggy would tie my hands behind my back, leaving me helpless on my knees, crawling to them between his long, muscular thighs as she rode him, her bottom right in my face as I took him in, to suck on his balls and lick just where I was told until they came together in a mutual climax and I was left dizzy with need and begging for my own release.

I would have screamed the house down if I hadn't been biting my lip; my climax was that strong as I imagined how it would be. As it was I was left gasping for breath so hard I was sure she would have heard, leaving my face hot with embarrassment as I came slowly down from my peak, a peak that in my imagination I hadn't even reached.

5

I spent most of the week analysing my own desires, something I'd done many times before, and while I'd at least partially comes to terms with my sexuality I couldn't claim to fully understand it. When it came to sexual fantasy, it was as if I was always driven to want the opposite to my normal needs. Where I hate being restricted, particularly by male chauvinism, I wanted to be tied up by a man of uncompromising virility. Where I like to make the decisions, I wanted that right taken away from me, so that I would have no choice but to do as I was told.

As I knew well, a fantasy does not necessarily reflect a desire for the same reality, far from it. The thought of actually putting myself in the sort of position I fantasised about was laughable, absurd, although there were elements it was tempting to at least try, especially being tied up, just in a situation where I could have absolute trust in my partner.

There was more too. For a long time I had accepted the very private streak of sexual submission within me, but Tiggy seemed to bring it out, just as she brought out the social insecurity I hadn't felt since I graduated. Did that imply an element of lesbianism in my sexual make-up, or was it simply that she represented a link with the sort of men I liked to fantasise over? Was it her I wanted, or something she could provide?

While invigilating a mock exam for all the third year

biology students I tried to gain a deeper understanding of myself by imagining situations, many of them outrageous, and gauging my own reaction. Unfortunately my feelings were invariably ambivalent, which really didn't help, and also inconsistent. My first thought was of how it would feel to kiss Tiggy mouth to mouth, which brought curiosity and a touch of embarrassment. My second was of how it would feel to hold her breasts, which again brought curiosity, but also a sense of self-deprecation for imagining taking such a liberty. My third was of how it would be to go down for her, which filled me with confusion and shock, but also a feeling that it would be somehow appropriate. Finally I conjured up the same image I'd come over on the Sunday night, which provoked a very different reaction, a sense of excitement and privilege, as if receiving some great honour. By then the thought of kissing her or touching her breasts seemed rather indifferent.

I was no nearer to drawing any firm conclusions, but I was so aroused I could barely sit still. A moment of looking out over the sea of earnest faces calmed me a little, but also put a wicked thought into my head. I was behind a solid desk, my legs tucked well under, the lower portion of my body invisible, the door at the far end of the room. All I needed to do was tug up my skirt a little and I would be able to play with myself then and there, a deliciously improper thought.

Too improper, outrageous, unthinkable, to masturbate in the presence of sixty-two third year students, male and female, but impossibly compelling. It would also allow me to continue my experiment, to see if the thought of kneeling down between Tiggy's open legs and bringing her to heaven under my tongue was enough to help me to climax, or if I needed a man. No, it was out of the question for a senior lecturer at

Keynes to do anything so ... so silly and also debauched. I would think about something else.

Unfortunately my immediate situation was more or less neutral. Only a small proportion of the students were studying environmental biology and I knew the ability of each. Nor did the room give much scope for thought, a long rectangle with windows on one side and the sole decoration a series of posters on wetland habitat, every detail of which was already familiar. Studying the students themselves was a route to disaster, as my eyes would inevitably be drawn to the more attractive males, with inevitable results only a shade less embarrassing than thinking about going down for Tiggy Blackmore.

I tried film, and *I ♥ Huckabees*, which Robert and I had been to see on the Wednesday night. It had been amusing, especially the irony of self-examination leading to the question of whether it would be better simply to live on the surface of things without regard for deeper meaning. Certainly I'd been able to see myself in it, always questioning everything rather than simply accepting it on face value, just as I had to analyse my sexual fantasies instead of just admitting to myself that I wanted to kiss and lick at some magnificent male's balls as Tiggy Blackmore rode his cock, her bare bottom right in my face ...

Only by jerking myself back from the edge did I stop myself from sliding a hand up my skirt. My resolve had lasted rather under one minute, and something over an hour of exam time remained. There was only one thing for it, to wander around annoying the students by peering over their shoulders at what they were writing and, with luck, by the time I got back to my desk I would have cooled down, at least enough to make the end of the exam.

I wandered down one row and up the next, down the third and up the fourth, down the fifth, and back, with nowhere left to go and no calmer than before, trapped. Leaving the hall was out of the question; I couldn't keep walking up and down for the rest of the exam, so I was just going to have to sit down and be sensible, thinking of something else, anything other than lean, powerful thighs and the heavy, virile swell of a man's balls.

Again I told myself it was an impossible, foolish thing to do, not to mention risky. Only it wasn't. Nobody was paying any attention to me whatsoever, and they couldn't see anyway. All I needed to do was pretended to be studying the papers on my desk and bite my lip when I came. It would be so easy, just a few careful touches and I'd be there. I wouldn't even need to put my hand down the front of my knickers. At the very least I could test, just to see if it would be as easy as it seemed.

That was all I was going to do, just test, and maybe take the edge off my tension with a few well-placed finger strokes. I adjusted my position, rucking my skirt up a little so that I could touch myself. Just doing that sent a shiver right through me, an exhibitionist thrill that reminded me of how I'd imagined sex in front of Tiggy. It felt so good, so wonderfully improper, a million miles away from everything safe and predictable.

I touched, just gently, but it was like an electric shock, making my muscles tighten. My tummy was fluttering with apprehension, part of my mind was screaming at me not to do it, but I was, stroking myself through the material of my knickers with my excitement rising so fast I had to catch my breath. Still nobody was looking, every face set in deep attention, not one of them remotely interested in their invigilator.

Why should they be? What could Dr Hazel Jones possibly do that was of interest to them?

Had they known, they'd have been horrified, I was sure, and even as I teased myself I was full of shame for what I was doing. That didn't stop me and I let my mind go back to what I'd thought of before, going down on my knees for Tiggy and whether that was enough, or if I needed a man. I was so close I wasn't sure if I needed anything but my own touch, but it would be nicer to add a little spice.

I picked up a piece of paper, shielding my face and pretending to study it, my fingers now pressed firmly in and moving in quick little circles, nearly there. Briefly I thought of how it would be if all the students knew, how wonderfully liberating it would be to have to masturbate openly in front of them, for whatever reason. It wasn't what I was supposed to be thinking about, but as I tried to focus on Tiggy once more the two fantasies merged into one and I had it to perfection.

She would make me go down, and she would do it in front of all her friends as a gesture of authority over me. I would be naked, my hands tied firmly behind my back, kneeling in front of her, my face pressed inbetween her thighs, my tongue busy, not for the physical contact, but to give her pleasure. That was it, so clear now that I wasn't trying to be rational about it. It wasn't Tiggy's body I wanted as such, but what she represented – to give in to somebody so confident, so sure, so horribly superior.

I only just bit my lip in time to prevent a sob from escaping my throat, now right on the edge as I pictured how it would be. Some little confrontation, maybe in a lecture hall, a packed lecture hall, and Tiggy answering me back. Tiggy telling me calmly but firmly that I needed to learn my place. Tiggy telling me what she was going to make me do, telling me to strip and watching as my clothes came off, ordering me to my knees, tying my hands tight behind my back to stop me shielding myself, pushing down her knickers under her skirt, sitting in front of me and opening her legs, demanding that I lick and keep licking until she'd come.

It took every ounce of my self-control to stop myself from making a noise as I came. The image of how I'd be was fixed firmly in my mind, me in abject, public submission to Tiggy, although my ecstasy was cut short with a jolt as I once more became fully aware of where I was.

My little piece of misbehaviour during the mock exam added considerably to my awareness of my own sexuality. For all that Tiggy was perfectly friendly and invariably polite, she represented everything I wasn't and everything I'd set myself against, particularly the establishment. So, in different ways, did all the macho-men – the stuck-up landowners, the crude farm boys, my archetypal males, all the figures from my fantasies.

That tied in well with the idea of finding it appealing to surrender the control I exercised in day-to-day life, and also that of shedding any sense of sexual guilt because I had no say in what was done. In turn, given that I wanted to be restrained, it made sense for it to be done by those I found most attractive sexually rather than in real life. After all, just because somebody turns me on doesn't mean I have to like them, or *vice versa*.

I felt I'd made an important step in understanding my sexuality and could therefore cope with my feelings more effectively. It was also going to help me express them in greater depth and detail, if only privately, because I had no intention of stopping. After all, this was purely fantasy.

The temptation to express those same dark desires in a more solid form had also grown stronger. If Tiggy could express herself so boldly, why shouldn't I? True, many aspects of my fantasy life were unacceptable in real life or even downright impossible, but others were not. For one thing I wanted to try sex while in restraint, preferably outdoors with my hands tied behind my back, which has always been my favourite. It was just a question of finding the opportunity.

Saturday was clear and fine, perfect for us, if also for the hunt, yet for once we actually needed them to succeed in order to achieve our aims. That worried me, as I'd never found it easy to come to terms with making a sacrifice of principle for the sake of the long-term good. Yet it was clearly the right thing to do, and possibly I would be able to intervene at the crucial moment, although I knew that would take exceptional courage.

The Breckland and Fen was meeting at the Black Cock in Wilton Parva, so we stayed well clear, except for a new member who was in the pub itself with his mobile phone to tell us which direction they set off in. It was amusing to imagine their relief at the absence of protestors for the first time in years, and I could hope that they'd be too arrogant to wonder why. The rest of us gathered in a lay-by outside Mildenhall, five couples in three cars, giving us the best chance of getting to where we were needed in time.

Paul had done his homework, sending in two members of the Cambridge saboteurs who weren't going to be recognised to pick up gossip in the local pubs. Sarah had also done a lot, walking miles on her day off in order to identify worthwhile locations, and she had jabbed a finger down in the middle of the map as soon as Robert had spread it out on the bonnet of his car.

'This is where I'll be. There's an earth here, and here, so I stand a good chance of getting to either one.'

Robert shook his head.

'How do you know they'll even go that way? Wouldn't it be better to stay with the cars?'

'No. Two of us should cover the most likely spots, leaving the others in cars to move quickly if need be. The other likely place is right over here, where some bloke who keeps chickens has been complaining about a fox, so they might well go there. You and Hazel had better cover that.'

She'd moved her finger to a great blank area on the map, well to the west of where the hunt would be starting. It seemed somewhat out of the way, but Sarah had already moved on, explaining to the others which roads to wait on. We were going to be deep in the fens, with broad stretches of water cutting us off to the south and west. If the hunt did come our way we would have a good chance of getting close, but the land was uncomfortably open.

I was already feeling nervous as we climbed back into Paul's car, and wishing I'd been paying attention during the meeting and stuck to my original intention of giving up active participation. It was too late to back out, and there did seem to be a realistic chance of getting that all-important footage, but I knew I'd be perfectly happy with a long, dull afternoon spent kicking my heels in the fens.

Paul dropped us off near Feltwell, leaving us to follow a long, arrow-straight footpath along the top of a minor dyke, with the flat brown and green fields stretching away in every direction to the distant woods behind us, and with the towers of Ely Cathedral hazy with distance in front. We had every right to be there, and looked no different to any other couple out for a Saturday afternoon walk, yet I found myself jumping even at the sight of a tractor in the far corner of a field. Robert was no better, talking to himself as much as to me as he psyched himself up for possible confrontation.

'What matters is that we get the footage, and we need to be close enough.'

'I'd rather be on the opposite side of a large river, if it's all the same.'

'That's unlikely to be practical.'

'I was joking, Robert. Seriously, it's so open here we'd have no chance of filming anything without being seen. Our only chance of success would be to pretend to be hunt supporters and hope nobody challenges us.'

'That's a thought. Do you think we could get away with it?'

'We have to try.'

'We do. Where shall we station ourselves? We need to be high enough to see, but we need some cover.'

'Not if we're pretending to be hunt followers, but maybe in that group of trees for the time being.'

I pointed to where I meant, a stand of tall white poplars rising up among dense blackthorn and elder scrub. There was still a faint mist hanging over the fields, with the dykes and trees rising above it to play curious tricks with the perspective. Our own dyke ran across the back of the copse, creating an ideal place to look out from, with the bank partially hidden by trees and shrouded in mist but with a clear view of anything approaching across miles of open fields. Down among the trees it was a different matter, with thick undergrowth and the dyke creating a crescent-shaped space of long, soft grass with the poplars rising from it as stiff and regular as sentinels. Robert gave a nod of satisfaction as he looked around.

'This is perfect, and any fox chased in our direction is almost certain to go to ground here.'

'Yes, as long as we're not too obvious. Perhaps we should stay in one corner? After all, we're likely to hear them long before we seem them.'

'That's true.'

We moved to the end of the grove, where the black-thorn thinned a little and a section of the barbed wire fence surrounding the field showed between the trunks. Hanging from one section of the fence was something completely mundane to most people, something barely to be registered, but to me an important part of many, many fantasies – a length of bailer twine.

I allowed myself a private smile at the thought of what could be done with the twine and the elaborate possibilities for fantasy offered by my situation. That was all, with more important work to be done, and I climbed back to the top of the dyke to scan the fields. Not a single human being was visible, only the roof of the tractor we'd seen earlier beyond a hedge and, well to the south, the upper works of pleasure boats moving along the Ouse, a peculiar sight as they were above the level of the fields.

My phone went. It was Sarah, to say that the hunt had moved off to the south, which made it difficult to be sure of their intentions. I scrambled back down to tell Robert, who had made himself comfortable on the rusting carcass of a tractor in among the blackthorn. As I approached he looked up from *The Ragged Trousered Philanthropists*, a book he never seemed to tire of re-reading. The engine housing of the old tractor was still largely intact, and with the wheels gone it made as convenient a seat as I was going to get. I sat down on it rather gingerly, half expecting the entire thing to collapse beneath me.

'They're headed south from Wilton Parva, on a track parallel to the B1112.'

'So they could go either way?'

'Yes, but it will be awkward if they go south of the Ouse.'

'Where's the nearest bridge?'

He unfolded the map, peering at it for a while before he spoke again.

'Brandon Bank, it looks like. Maybe we should go there?'

'We'd have to cross the dyke too. Does it join the river?'

'I'm not sure, but it curves back on itself. We'd have to walk maybe two miles east before we could cross.'

'And very likely run straight into them. Let's wait here, at least until we get another call.'

We waited, for ten minutes, and twenty, before I lost patience and rang Sarah. She was no wiser than we were and hadn't heard from any of the cars. Another half-hour passed and I'd begun to get restless, climbing the bank every few minutes to look out across the countryside, the very placidity of which seemed to taunt me. Finally Sarah rang again, to say the hunt had been spotted crossing the bottom of Wangford Fen, directly towards her position. Immediately my tension had begun to drain away, to leave me both relieved and disappointed. Robert looked up.

'Sarah?'

'Yes. They're moving towards her. It doesn't look as if anything's going to happen now.'

'Probably not.'

I didn't answer him, feeling slightly irritable and somewhat without purpose. We'd been there over an hour and not seen a single person, while the sun had risen high enough to burn the last of the mist off the fields and the day was growing warm. We had water, but no food, and the bowl of muesli I'd snatched for breakfast was beginning to feel inadequate. Robert was deep in his book and I knew that his conversation would be distracted at best. Lost for anything to do, I wandered over to the section of bare fence, twisting the length of bailer twine around one finger as I stared out across the empty field.

The copse was pleasantly close to the setting for so many of my fantasies – lonely, rural and invested with the sense of antagonism farmland had brought me since my first forays as a hunt saboteur. It was very easy indeed to people the landscape with elegant, harsh-faced huntsmen and burly farm boys, just the sort I liked to imagine myself surrendering too.

What I had was Robert, his mind as deep in his book as his nose, lost in the inequities of early twentieth century class politics and moral indignation at the treatment of workers. My own ideas for the treatment of workers were rather different, and would have cheered them up no end, offering to let them do with me as they pleased, just so long as my hands were tied to make sure I had little choice about the details. They'd have to be the right sort of workers, of course, not so much the oppressed urban sort as sturdy rural landsmen, the sort who went on hunts and voted Conservative, the sort who'd take immense pleasure in putting a left-wing university lecturer through her paces.

The thought made me shiver, of how much pleasure they'd take in me and how thoroughly they'd enjoy me before they'd had their fill. However many there were, maybe a dozen or more. I'd have to satisfy them all, doing whatever they demanded, or if I was tied securely enough, maybe across the engine of the old tractor, they could simply do as they liked, one after another, again and again and again ...

So could Robert, if I could only manage to suggest to him that tying a woman up when she wanted to be tied up didn't automatically make him a prospective Tory candidate. Yet even then he might well do it, if I made it very clear it was what I really wanted, and it would be nice to feel myself physical helpless while knowing I could trust him absolutely not to go beyond my limits.

I spent a long time in indecision, biting my lip as my thoughts moved between desire to have my hands tied for sex and the certainty that even if Robert did comply the experience would lack something. Yet I always used my imagination when we had sex, so it wouldn't be so very different, while at least my hands would be tied for real. At last I decided to do it and untied the length of bailer twine from the fence with trembling fingers and a fluttering stomach.

He was as before, perched on the ancient tractor seat, one knee lifted to balance his elbow as he read. The pose captured his thoughtful, studious manner, one of the things that had attracted me to him in the first place. He was good-looking, in a rather tame way, but with us it had always been a meeting of minds first and foremost, made easy by his need to please. I stepped close, twisting the twine back and forth between my fingers and wondering how I should put the question. Perhaps his way.

'Would ... would you like to make love?'

'Here?'

He looked astonished, to put it mildly. I came close, to let our cheeks touch and kiss his neck, feeling the slight roughness of his skin where his bristles had begun to come through and catching his scent. He reacted, putting the book down carefully on the engine casing and kissing me in return. I let my mouth open to his, feeling that slow but sure arousal which comes with knowing what is going to happen with a familiar partner. This time I wanted more, and broke away just as his fingers had begun to tease the nape of my neck and the curve of one breast. At the very least I had to ask, and I was sure the best way was to be firm and confident.

'I want you to do me a little favour. Don't say anything, just do it.'

'OK, what is it?'

I swallowed hard, struggling to get the words out as I offered him the length of bailer twine.

'Tie my hands behind my back.'

He looked incredulous, as if I'd suggested we join the hunt or eat at McDonald's. I felt my heart sink and an awful, sickly sense of disappointment and shame began to bubble up in my stomach. Then he nodded.

'If that's what you want.'

'I . . . I just thought it might be fun.'

Again he nodded, far from sure of himself and no doubt thinking I'd gone mad, but he was going to do it, and my heart was absolutely hammering. He took the twine and I turned around, crossing my wrists behind my back in a gesture I'd imagined so, so many times. Now it was real, for the first time, and I closed my eyes to savour every last instant of the experience.

I felt his fingers on my skin, holding me in place, and the twine tickling, then I tensed as he twisted it around one wrist, then the other. A sharp jolt hit me, something not so very far from orgasm as I felt it, my wrists now linked, and linked securely as he took more turns with the twine, lashing my arms firmly into place with a bond far too strong for me to break.

A knot, and it was done, my arms were fastened securely behind my back, and I was no longer able to use my hands, a sensation so powerful that shiver after shiver of pleasure was running through my body. I already felt in need of him inside me, an extraordinarily small time after we'd first kissed, but I didn't want to ask. I wanted him to take control, to do all the things to me I liked to imagine. My voice was hoarse as I spoke.

'Just enjoy yourself, anyway you like.'

I took a couple of steps back towards the tractor, because I knew where I wanted to be and he could hardly be expected to read my mind. Walking felt deliciously awkward, a little off balance so that I had to take tiny steps. I'd always imagined how good it would feel to be helpless, but never realised just how strong the feeling was, with my body flushed hot and my mind teeming with emotions. As I laid myself down across the engine casing of the tractor they grew stronger still. So often I'd imagined the same vulnerable position, with a man standing over me, a man who knew he could do just as he liked and I would do just as I was told. Surely even Robert would have to take advantage of me when I was not only willing and helpless, but had offered myself?

'What would you like me to do, darling?'

'Take advantage of me, however you please.'

He nodded doubtfully as I looked back over my shoulder, hesitant, far too hesitant, but then his hands had gone to my hips. Just his touch was electric, knowing he could take my jeans down for me and there was nothing I could do to stop him, my knickers too, and take full advantage of my bare bottom, explore me, rub himself between my cheeks, even smack them, all deliciously inappropriate acts.

'Lift up a little.'

I obeyed immediately, raising my hips to let him get at my jeans button. He was going to do it, a wonderfully male act, to pull my trousers down and get straight to the heart of the matter without bothering about foreplay. I was ready though; I'd been ready since the moment he'd accepted the bailer twine and I'd known he would put me in bondage.

As his fingers found my fly I closed my eyes, concentrating everything on touch: the feel of the twine around my wrists rendering me helpless as I was exposed: the gentle release of pressure as he popped my button and again as my zip was drawn down; the feel of his fingers in the waistband of my jeans, and the cool air on my flesh as they were drawn slowly down, knickers and all.

I was bare, not in any casual way, but bare for sex, bare outdoors, tied up and in a thoroughly indecent pose, which there had to be at least a chance of somebody else seeing. If they did and it was a man I'd want them to join in, perhaps in my mouth as Robert took me from behind. Even a woman might have a little fun with me, if she was so inclined. What I thought didn't matter. I was tied up.

Robert was right behind me, adjusting my jeans and knickers around my legs, so that I could imagine exactly what he could see. He'd be growing hard, ready for me, he had to be, and I wanted him in my mouth. I wanted everything else too, all at once, to be held by my hair as I was made to lick and kiss and suck at his cock and balls, to be taken roughly from behind, long and hard, to have him forget all about what was appropriate and really make the best of me. He could even indulge himself in ways completely out of the question for any self-respecting modern woman, making me lick below his balls or telling me to pee so that he could watch, spanking my bottom, anything. Maybe, just maybe, he would even be tempted to try and push his cock into the tight hole between my cheeks.

A sob broke from my throat at the thought, just as he stepped around the tractor. I opened my eyes. His hand was on his fly, his face set in doubt but also in unmistakable lust as he spoke.

'Would you like to . . .'

He didn't finish, but I knew what he meant and I was already nodding my head urgently. One nervous glance around the copse and he had pulled down his zip. Another and he had taken out his cock, already half-swollen in his excitement as he offered himself to me. I took him in, sucking eagerly with my feelings soaring higher than ever. As he grew in my mouth I closed my eyes once more and let my mind run, already in need of my climax and wishing I could touch myself, but so, so glad I couldn't.

It was the most glorious of situations, bent across a rusting tractor in the countryside with my trousers pulled down and a man's penis swelling in my mouth. Perhaps it should have been some rough and ready farmhand instead of my caring, gentle Robert, but his cock was every bit as good. It was only a shame there weren't two of him, or four, or eight, to take me in every way possible again and again.

That was how I wanted it, placed just as I was, bare and vulnerable, for the enjoyment of a whole string of men, and for the last one, the very last one, to reach around and bring me to ecstasy under his fingers in front of all his friends, even as he came himself. Robert's voice broke into my fantasy, gruff and excited as he began to tug as his now rock-hard cock.

'Like this, like I'm doing it?'

I shook my head and he pulled out immediately, leaving me panting for breath before I could answer.

'No. Go behind me, and don't ask, just do it, everything, but make me come!'

He went, disappearing from view around the tractor as my mouth set into a happy smile. I knew he would do it, he always did, and he knew how. With luck he'd also interpret 'everything' as an offer to be thoroughly rude with me. His hands found my hips, I felt the hot, hard shaft of his cock touch my bottom, and my stomach went tight in mingled apprehension and an overpowering desire as I wondered if he would really dare to put it up.

I felt him take hold, his knuckles touching my skin, pushing his cock lower, just inches from my vulnerable bottom hole, and lower still, to push deep inside me with one long, easy thrust. With that I was in heaven, tied up and taken from behind, fantasy made reality after so long, too long. As he began to push I was already gasping, my muscles tight with ecstasy, my whole world focused on my firmly bound wrists, the feel of my partially naked body, and of his erection inside me. I cried out, on the edge of orgasm because every push was pressing me to the smooth old paint of the tractor casing, but it wasn't enough, not quite.

The need to touch myself was agonising, but I couldn't, I was tied up, and that made the need stronger still, until I was writhing in frustrated ecstasy, showing my feelings as I never had with a man before. I could barely think, but words were tumbling from my lips as crazy, heated demands, to be brought to climax, to have my bottom spanked, to be sodomised.

He never spoke, but his hand curled under me and he was doing it, clutching at me, clumsy in his own urgency, but it was enough, just the way a rough young farm boy might have done it, to make me come more for his own pleasure and the amusement of his friends than for my sake. What if the hunt came? Then it might happen for real. They'd make short work of Robert, and there would be nothing I could do about it. They would have me, and he'd be made to watch. They'd give me what I really needed, and they would sodomise me.

I gasped out as it hit me, so loud I startled birds from the trees above us, and again as wave after wave of ecstasy washed through me. My wrists were pulled tight in my bonds, to really bring home the feeling of being tied. His thrusts had grown frantic, jamming me against the tractor over and over again as I shook in orgasm, with my head burning with the image of how I was, my wrists tied hard behind my back, my jeans and knickers pulled down, bent over an old tractor with a man inside me as I came.

I very nearly fainted and, even though as I'd come I'd been imagining the same situation with a dozen farmhands, I was immediately very grateful indeed that it was only Robert. He could be guaranteed to look after me, not to rough me up too much for one thing, and also to untie me when I asked.

Except that he couldn't. I'd been tugging at my bonds so hard as I came that the knot had been pulled tighter, too tight for his fingernails to get it open. I did need to get up, because it was beginning to hurt, but I could see the funny side of it too, laughing as Robert fought to get the knot open with increasing impatience and consternation, until I heard something that put my heart into my mouth – a hunting horn.

Suddenly the very thing that had a moment before been what I desired more than anything else in the world had become a terrifying and extremely unwelcome reality. They were coming towards us; they had to be, because there was nowhere else to go. They were coming towards us and I was bent over a tractor with my trousers around my ankles and my hands tied behind my back. OK, so they wouldn't actually do what I'd imagined, but that was only so much consolation.

'Untie me!'

'I can't!'

'Cut the twine!'

'What with.'

'How should I know? Just do it!'

He began to panic, jerking at my bonds with his fingers and then with his teeth. The horn sounded again, nearer, and I caught the sound of dogs, familiar enough but now terrifying. Suddenly I realised what he could do.

'Smash the water bottle, use the glass!'

'But the litter . . .'

'Sod the fucking litter! Do it!'

He ran for our things and I struggled to get to my feet, almost succeeding, only to trip over my own jeans and go headlong, face down on the ground, bottom up and half naked with the sounds of the dogs growing louder, and louder still. The first thing I saw was the fox, a streak of rusty brown as it dashed in among the poplars just yards ahead of me. I will swear it gave me a look of surprise before it disappeared up the bank, and then Robert was with me.

So were the hounds, and even at that awful moment I felt sympathy for the fox, although a great deal more for myself. One burst through the bushes right at me, and for one truly horrible moment I thought it was going to go for me, its breath foul in my face, its tongue wet and sticky as it began to lick me. I was babbling at it to stop, and also for Robert to cut the twine, but it was only as I rolled over onto my back that I realised why he was being so slow. He hadn't even smashed the bottle, but was using the camcorder to film the swarming dogs in the main part of the woods.

'Robert! Help!'

'Hang on ... hang on ...'

He stopped filming, snatched at the bottle and smashed it against the trunk of a poplar. Taking the jagged neck, he had cut my bonds in an instant, only to go straight back to filming as I jumped to my feet. My fingers were numb, making it nearly impossible to get my knickers up, let alone my jeans, but I did it, and not a moment too soon. I caught a flash of pink, saw a great bay horse jump the fence, another, and the huntsmen were pouring into the woods, with the hounds now streaming up the bank. Of the fox there was no sign.

I don't know what it was, maybe sheer adrenaline, but I was running immediately, straight towards the pack. An angry shout rang out to one side, but I didn't even slow, scrambling up the bank to where a great mass of hounds were milling around, expecting to see a mess of bloody fur among them at any instant. I heard one splash, another, a third as the hounds took to the water. When I'd reached the top of the bank I could see the fox too, streaking away across the fields on the far side of the dyke.

He wasn't the only one. Robert was running along the top, back the way we'd come, as fast as his legs could carry him, the camera clutched in his hand.

They'd seen him, but it was me the leading huntsman was shouting at as I turned to face him, drawing in my breath to give back whatever he had to say to me with interest.

Let there be no mistake. There is an enormous gulf between fantasy and reality.

6

I wasn't entirely happy about Robert's behaviour, but there was no denying that he'd achieved what we'd set out to do, and with everybody else praising our success it was hard to be resentful. For whatever reason, the hunt had no sooner reached the edge of the Breckland woods than they had turned back, leaving Sarah lying in wait for nothing and the others travelling in entirely the wrong direction.

Possibly they had flushed out the fox, but they'd certainly been chasing it as they entered our area, and with no saboteurs about and nothing but open fields around them, they had let the hounds have their head. The fox had swum the dyke, but it was our presence that had saved it in the end, with the huntsmen calling the hounds back before they could swim across because the Master had recognised me and knew who I was.

I'd been so pumped up I hadn't even been scared as I stood alone on the dyke with the hounds milling around me and ringed in by an ever increasing number of huntsmen and followers. Only afterwards had the reaction set in, and we'd had to stop the car for Sarah to take me in among the trees and hold me while I was sick. Even at that moment there was a glow of admiration in her eyes.

The footage was as good as we could possibly have hoped for. Robert had caught the fox as it ran into the wood and panned around to film the hunt as they came towards the copse, leaving no doubt whatsoever that they were hunting with a pack of hounds as defined, and forbidden, by law. As we watched the playback on his computer I also realised that had I not tripped over myself the shot would have included me, stark naked from waist to ankles and with my wrists tied.

By the time I got home I was exhausted physically, but still buzzing mentally. A chat with Tiggy over a bottle of wine would have been ideal, but she was nowhere to be seen. A note on the kitchen table informed me that she had gone up to Brancaster, so I contented myself with a solitary glass and retired to bed with Flann O'Brien.

In the morning I had begun to pay for my exertions of the day before. I had several bruises and my legs ached, but far worse were the two circular marks on my wrists, the only possible explanation for which was that they'd been bound. It was the hottest day of the year so far, really quite summery, but I was obliged to choose a long sleeved blouse with loose cuffs to hide the evidence of my misbehaviour.

There was no denying the pleasure in the constant reminder of what I'd done, but it was also an irritation, and led me to question my own personal responsibility. Not that I'd done anything wrong, but I'd chosen a bad time to do it. There never would have been a good time, at least not during term, and I'd had no idea the marks would show, but it would have been hard to choose a worse moment.

I'd be angling for a place as external examiner for appropriate PhD theses, which would not only bring in extra income but had the potential to be a good career move. On the Tuesday I was to meet a Dr Davis-Brown at Merton College in Cambridge, a man whose work I'd been reading when I was an undergraduate myself, which made the prospect a little daunting. Not that it was a formal interview, but he clearly had a great deal of influence and I was determined to make a good impression. A thorough knowledge of his own work was clearly a good start, which meant going back over old issues of journals in the library.

Being a close friend of Sarah's was an advantage, as it meant I could stay much later than would normally have been possible, but again I had to be extremely careful she didn't see my wrists, as I knew she would have been horrified. Once I'd finished she insisted on treating me to a Thai meal in town on the strength of my performance on Sunday, with Robert's contribution conveniently, and typically, forgotten.

I accepted, and it was nearly midnight before I got home, to find that Tiggy had still not returned, although her door was wide open with her diary lying on her desk, so obvious she might almost have put it there deliberately. As usual I was tempted, but this time I was tired enough to overcome the urge, while hours spent reading about oceanic plankton biomass and listening to Sarah's conversation had left me anything but aroused.

In the morning I was up early to make a careful selection of clothes. Dr Davis-Brown's first paper had been published in nineteen fifty-nine, which put him in his seventies, so it seemed likely he would be a traditionalist. A skirt therefore seemed sensible, although as I hunted through my wardrobe I could imagine Sarah's disapproving look for attempting to create an attractive impression with an elderly Cambridge don, or any other man for that matter.

After some thought I decided on my woollen skirt suit, which was both smart yet quiet, also a plain white blouse and, in a moment of mild humour, blue tights, the nearest I had to stockings. The woman reflected in my mirror didn't look all that like me at all, unless it was the last time I'd been to a funeral, but as nearly as I could judge it would be what he was expecting.

I'd taken a copy of one of his lighter works, *The Earth's Powerhouse: Photosynthesis in Marine Phytoplankton* to read on the train, and that kept me busy all the way to Cambridge, where I quickly found Merton among the older colleges at the centre of town, and Dr Davis-Brown's room on the first floor of a squat tower. It wasn't my first time at Cambridge by any means, but the sense of pomp and antiquity was still so very different from the light and air of Keynes that it was impossible not to feel out of place, even somewhat detached from reality, so much so that I nearly ran into a student as I entered the tower. It was quite a shock, as I'd been looking up at a moon-faced gargoyle carved at the apex of the arched doorway and suddenly found myself faced with a pale face, his mouth slightly open in surprise. Both of us apologised simultaneously, and I was smiling for my own imagination as I knocked on the door.

'Come.'

Dr Davis-Brown was seated behind a huge brown keyhole desk, his round red face immediately recognisable from the frontispiece of his book, although his hair had declined to a white fringe, making it seem as if he wore a monk's tonsure and adding considerably to the medieval feel of the place. He looked puzzled and I quickly checked my watch to make sure I did have the right time before speaking.

'Good morning, Dr Davis-Brown. I am Dr Hazel Jones; I believe you are expecting me?'

'Dr Jones? Ah, yes, absolutely ... do take a seat. I expect you drink sherry, or perhaps a glass of port?'

There didn't seem to be an option for neither.

'Sherry, please.'

'Splendid. I'll have a whisky splash, myself.'

There were two huge armchairs, both upholstered in shiny leather that had once been green but was now cracked and faded by light to a reticulated yellow. I took one, waiting as he moved to a sideboard and poured the drinks. To judge by his greeting he hadn't even realised I was female, which in turn implied he hadn't read my CV, hardly a good start. At least he seemed friendly enough, beaming broadly as he passed me a large glass full almost to the brim with a nut-brown sherry. Thinking of the horrible sticky substance my great-aunt Ida served at Christmas, I took a careful sip, to find it dry and sharp, also rich and heady with alcohol. He took a swallow of his own drink before speaking again.

'You're a lecturer at Keynes Polytechnic, I believe?'

'Yes, I've been Senior Lecturer for three years, although of course we're a university now.'

He shook his head.

'Everywhere seems to be these days. Still, I've been looking at some of your papers . . .'

He paused to fan out some of the clutter on his desk, peering close before extracting a paper. It was one of mine, a recent one, and as much political as scientific as it had been commissioned by DEFRA as part of their study to make farming more environmentally friendly. He was frowning as he read over the synopsis to himself, but I couldn't be sure if it was disapproval or simply short sight. At last he nodded.

'Hmm, yes, you don't seem to be a great believer in knowledge for its own sake?'

I hesitated, pushing back the desire to try and say the right thing in favour of my real view.

'I believe in knowledge as a tool for improvement, by which I don't necessarily mean conventional human progress. Having said that, I think it is a mistake to concentrate purely on areas of research for which the benefits are plain. To take an example from your own work, your data on ostracod populations in the Barents Sea might not have been considered to have any human application, but it now forms an important part of the overall data on changes in biodiversity and species distribution as they relate to oceanic temperatures and possibly global warming.'

'They do? Extraordinary! That would be from the work I did with old Heath.'

'Heath and Davis-Brown: 1962, also Davis-Brown, Cook and Roberts: 1969.'

He gave me a brief but searching look, making me wonder if he wasn't putting on an image of the vague and aged don on purpose, perhaps as some sort of test. His most recent paper suggested otherwise, that he was in full command of his faculties if not particularly in tune with modern thought. He chuckled.

'I see you've done your homework, my dear.'

I felt a jolt of irritation at the familiar address but reminded myself that a man of his age was likely to be unreconstructed, for which I should make allowances. He put my paper down and took another swallow of whisky and soda, apparently lost in thought, only to speak again.

'Do you like oysters, to eat I mean?'

It couldn't have been more irrelevant, and took me completely aback, but I managed to answer more or less by instinct.

'I've never eaten one. I'm a vegetarian.'

He shook his head, this time in clear disapproval. My heart sank, my disappointment tempered with anger at the possibility of being dismissed over something so arbitrary, but he spoke again.

'So you're going to be examining young Paddon?'

It was more a statement than a question, and again caught me completely wrong-footed before I could recover myself.

'I, er ... I would hope so, if you think I'm a suitable candidate?'

He looked surprised.

'I can't imagine why you wouldn't be. Yes, Paddon, Simmons and Ray I have you down for. I do hope that's OK?'

'Um ... yes, absolutely, of course.'

Again I had to take a moment to adjust, as it now seemed I'd already had the job. He went on.

'Paddon you'll be particularly interested in as his work relates to your own, at least tangentially. He's comparing current levels of biodiversity with past records across a remarkably broad range of habitats. Quite a bit to bite off, but he's a bright lad and it seems to be going well. Very keen too. You just missed him as it happens, a pity, although I suppose if we are to be absolutely certain of our ethics it's best that you haven't been introduced.'

'Yes, quite.'

'That's settled then. Can I offer you lunch, if you are prepared to dine in the company of us wicked carnivores?'

It had been the most peculiar interview, but I seemed to have been taken on, beforehand even, which was what mattered, and no doubt the full arrangements would be made in due course. Dr Davis-Brown also seemed pleasant enough, if rather old-fashioned, but I wasn't sure if he exaggerated his eccentricity or not. In the end I'd found myself rather charmed by him, and my initial defensiveness had entirely evaporated. No doubt he was very much of the establishment, and no doubt he did hold many opinions in opposition to my own, but it was hard not to be drawn in by his friendly manner. On the train back I even allowed myself a brief foray into fantasy, wondering if he was the sort who liked to spank women for pleasure, and how it would feel to be put across his knee, but the idea was simply too outrageous to take in.

I arrived back in time to get an hour's work down in the labs. Back at home there was still no sign of Tiggy, which worried me enough to consider calling her. I didn't in the end, not wishing to seem to be invading her personal space by playing the old mother hen, and called Robert instead. He wasn't answering, either at home or on his mobile, which left me feeling at something of a loose end.

A glass of wine seemed like an excellent idea, and I put a bottle of Soave in the fridge while I made a bowl of pasta with red pesto sauce for my dinner. I ate slowly, but still seemed to have finished in no time at all, leaving me seated at the kitchen table with my glass of wine and the house oddly empty. There was plenty to do, but nothing urgent and I lacked inspiration, perhaps in reaction to having achieved something so easily after imagining it would be difficult.

I began to put things together for recycling in a rather half-hearted manner, first glass, then tins, then paper, which was what led me into Tiggy's room. Everything was exactly as it had been before, so she clearly hadn't been back during the day, her diary included, as big and blue and tempting as ever. I immediately knew that I was not going to be able to get through the evening without looking inside, not unless I went out and came back so late and so exhausted I'd fall straight to sleep.

Even then it might not work, and with a strong flush of guilt I decided to get it over with, promising myself only that I would avoid reading any of those dates on which she might have mentioned me. That was tricky, in that we'd known each other for the whole of the year, but easy enough as she never seemed to record anything other than her sexual exploits. Just as nervous and just as guilty as the first time, I turned back the cover, a few pages in from the beginning.

February 13th Monday

Went to see Star Wars with Gareth. Boring boys own stuff, so I made him come up to the back row and sucked his cock instead.

That was it, and while the idea of Tiggy taking Gareth in her mouth in the back row of a cinema was exciting, it seemed a little tame by comparison with what I knew she sometimes got up to. More than anything I wanted to know if she'd let herself be tied up at all. After my own experience with Robert it was more intriguing than ever, and sure to fill my head with all sorts of exciting ideas. The next day would be Valentine's, which had to be promising. Sure enough.

February 14th Tuesday

Valentine's Day! Only five cards.

Only five cards? Only! I'd never had more than two, even as a teenager. Then again, this was Tiggy.

And two I don't know about, so it won't be too hard to keep my promise. Saul was easy cause he was taking me out, so I did him in the car park behind Blues Notes.

Blues Notes was a club in Bury, a popular venue with students, although I'd never been there. Again it was intriguing to think of Tiggy and Saul enjoying sex among the shadows between the cars, but not what I was looking for. More intriguing was her promise, and exactly what it entailed. I turned another page.

February 15th Wednesday

Gareth's turn. I know he had Monday night, but a promise is a promise and I was feeling horny. Met him at the Blue Boar and took him back to my room. Quite drunk, so I gave him a long, slow striptease and peed in my sink in front of him before going down. He got dirty with me and wanted to do it in my face, which was OK.

I swallowed hard. So this was the shy, good-natured sportsman she said was easy going about her seeing other men, enjoying watching her pee and wanting to come in her face, something so outrageous I didn't know whether to be angry or aroused. She was so casual about it too, as if doing something it was hard to see as anything other than degrading was of no great consequence at all. I shook myself as I turned another page, wondering if it was me who was repressed or if Tiggy was suffering from some sort of sexual addiction.

February 16th Thursday

Found out who Valentine No 4 was from, Luke! Didn't even know he fancied me, and what about

Janice? What she doesn't know won't hurt her, I suppose, hee, hee!

Met Dean for lunch and gave him his in the loos at the labs, with people coming and going all the time we were at it. Took him ages, but good. I came three times! Met Luke as I was coming out of lectures and told him about my promise, hinting that I just might.

I did. He came round late and asked for it straight out. I wanted to make him wait, and to tease him a bit for being so cocky, but he just sat down in my chair and pulled it all out. He's that cute, what could I do? I sucked him.

We were going well when Janice came in. She really gave it to me, shouting and screaming and saying she was going to teach me a lesson. I kept trying to say sorry but she wouldn't take any notice and she made me lick her, right there, while he watched!

I knew they'd set it up right from the start, because her anger was really fake.

I read it again, and a third time, barely able to take in what I was seeing. Luke and Janice were both second year students, and had been a couple from the first week of the first year. He was certainly good-looking, tall with a slim, athletic body, and so was she, but if I could imagine him being cocksure and arrogant when it came to sex, she was a very different matter. I'd hardly ever heard her speak except to answer a question, and when I had it was in a quiet voice, as if expecting to be contradicted at every word. To picture her making the super confident Tiggy submit to her for rough, lesbian sex would have been impossible were it not for the last line.

Janice worshipped Luke, and I could think of plenty

of instances where women in love had done much more extreme things for the sake of a man, outrageous though it was. That would be it, a careful set-up by Luke so that he could watch two girls together, which is said to be the commonest of all male fantasies. It was still hard to take in, if only because it implied he had known Tiggy would do it, and she was not somebody to be bullied easily.

What had happened was disturbing too, for all that Tiggy had obviously enjoyed it. I knew her, and she wouldn't have done it otherwise, yet it was essentially sexual bullying, and as such utterly unacceptable. As her tutor it would be my responsibility as well, despite the fact that she hadn't complained.

Yet what could I do? I'd read it in her diary, not to mention that the thought of it was sending shivers down my spine. Ideally I would have rather it was Janice who'd been made to lick Tiggy and not the other way around or, better still, me. The idea was immensely arousing, and yet it also filled me with guilt for what had been done to Tiggy, conflicting emotions so strong I felt close to tears as I shut the diary.

Already I could picture how I would play the scene out as I masturbated, with Luke as Tiggy's boyfriend and me made to lick her in abject apology for sucking his cock. Yet I didn't want to do it and I wasn't sure I could, not when I felt so bad about it. It would only be fantasy in my head, it was true, but it would be drawn from an unacceptable reality, unacceptable for all Tiggy's apparent delight in it, extraordinary delight.

Could she really be that strong? I compared my own reaction in not completely dissimilar circumstances; my urgent fantasy desire to be taken by a large group of rough men while tied up and with no say in the matter against how I'd reacted when faced with an approximation of the reality, stood alone with the entire Breckland and Fen hunt around me. Fantasy had been intensely arousing, reality completely without sexual reference.

For Tiggy to have simply accepted what Janice had done to her suggested either that she was a natural victim and had tried to make her ordeal seem positive in an attempt to come to terms with it, or that she was strong that she could accept and enjoy the physical reality of the act while remaining mentally detached. Tiggy was no victim, so it had to be the latter, which left me in awe.

The only thing I could think of to do with myself was to have a large drink while I tried to come to terms with my own feelings. Having made sure the diary was exactly as I found it, I went back downstairs. The bottle of Soave was still three-quarters full, but it wasn't going to stay that way for long. I poured a glass and sat down, the bottle on the table in front of me, but had only just begun to put my thoughts in order when the doorbell rang.

It was a shock, adding to my guilty feelings and my embarrassment for what I'd been doing, so I was sure I was pink in the face as I hurried to the door, to find myself face to face with Dean, the man who Tiggy had given oral sex in the toilets at the labs. He was much as usual, in a pair of tatty jeans and his black leather bike jacket, the front open to show a plain white T-shirt stretched taut over well-defined muscles, which drew my gaze inexorably downwards until he spoke.

'Hi. Is Tiggy around? I know we're not supposed to knock and that, but she's not answering her mobile.'

'No, no, that's all right. She's with Saul, I think, somewhere up on the north coast.'

'Saul's off up Norwich. She going to be back?'

'Perhaps. I'm not sure. Would you like to come in? I've just opened a bottle of wine.'

He hesitated, then shrugged and turned back to retrieve his helmet from the handlebars of his bike. I wasn't even quite sure why I'd invited him in, save perhaps to save myself from my own reactions, but my stomach was fluttering badly as I shut the door and ushered him through to the kitchen. He was big, taller than I'd realised when seeing him at a distance, and broad-shouldered, undoubtedly manly, as was his smell, a touch of male and a touch of motorbike.

It felt strange, and a little daring, to be entertaining one of Tiggy's men. He was everything I'd have expected: tough, cool, perhaps exaggeratedly so in order to hide his unease; perhaps no more sure what to talk about that I was. As he glanced around the kitchen I poured him a glass of wine, which he took in his hand as if holding a tumbler.

'Nice place you've got here.'

'Thank you. Do sit down.'

He sat, and there was a moment of embarrassed silence, with me wondering exactly what I was doing and he no doubt wishing Tiggy would turn up and rescue him.

'Tiggy shouldn't be too long.'

I didn't know if it was true, but it was all I could think of to say beyond the sort of inconsequential small talk that would only make the atmosphere worse. Yet he didn't seem inclined to speak and I had to say something.

'Do you live locally?'

'Yeah, on the Cornridge.'

It was a new estate on the southern edge of town, not somewhere I'd been. Again he went silent. I hid a sigh behind my wine glass, wishing I didn't feel so awkward and wondering how Tiggy would have coped in the circumstances. To judge by her diary she'd have suggested sex, probably with rather more aplomb than I'd suggested a glass of wine. She made it seem so easy; while for all that he appealed to me I knew I could never do it at all, for fear of rejection, embarrassment, a sense that it would be inappropriate. Instead I sipped wine and watched the wall, wondering why it was that I could brave twenty men on horseback but not even hold a conversation with one in my own kitchen. In the end he spoke.

'You work at the poly, right?'

'We're a university now, but yes.'

'What's the difference?'

'Between a university and a polytechnic? The distinction used to be that universities were purely academic, offering study for disciplines such as philosophy, theology, and later law, medicine – the arts and sciences in general – while polytechnics focused on technical subjects with a vocational goal. The boundaries had already begun to blur before the change was made, and the academic world stills recognises a distinction, although I for one would argue that it's not a valid one.'

'Really they did it just to make the polys look better, yeah?'

'Not at all. For a long time now the focus of research has come to rest more on subjects with a clear application to humanity, such as my own subject, environmental biology, which has obvious benefits, while, say, entomology – which is the study of insects – has fewer unless they relate to crop pests and so forth. So universities were becoming more like polytechnics and polytechnics were becoming more like universities anyway.'

'Yeah, but it's all the same, isn't it, just money and status, just words? Why not call them all polytechnics?'

'It had to be one or the other.'

'It's all bollocks! Like in Nineteen Eighty-Four, where the Party twists everything so it means what they want and the proles feel good about it even though it's shit.'

'You've read Nineteen Eighty-Four? Sorry, I don't mean to be patronising.'

'Yeah. Tiggy said I should read it.'

I nodded, remembering how she'd compared the regime at her school with the Party. Again it seemed to me to be an exaggeration.

'I don't think it's entirely fair to compare our government with Orwell's Party.'

'Where's the difference?'

'Our system is nothing like as authoritarian! Yes, there are faults, but those are mainly hangovers from eighteen years of Tory rule, or from older repressive institutions, the Squirearchy, the Church, the Military.'

'What about all the cameras going up, and this zero tolerance bullshit?'

'Now there you're thinking like a stereotypical male. For a woman the cameras in town provide security, as does the extra street lighting. I was involved in both campaigns, and I'm proud of the results.'

'Yeah, right, I haven't got a problem with them being used for stuff like that, but it's like they find a good excuse to do it, like that, only that's not what they use it for, is it?'

'How do you mean?'

'Like Saul got an eighty-quid fine 'cause he got caught by that camera at the top of Anson Park, doing a right turn. It was three in the fucking morning!'

I was going to reply that Saul had broken the law but didn't, thinking of all the minor breaches of the law I'd carried out over the years, always justified by the cause. Saul had no cause, but he had done no harm either. Dean went on, now with a shade of aggression in his voice.

'You middle-class types are all the same...'

That was too much.

'Excuse me, but I am not middle class, and I resent your generalisation. Also, I've spent most of my life campaigning for liberal causes!'

'Yeah, sure, the ones you're into, the ones you get something out of,'

'I'm sorry, but that's not true at all. For instance, I, personally, have nothing at all to gain from the ban on hunting with hounds.'

'That's 'cause you hate nobby types, isn't it? Blokes riding around in red jackets with la-di-dah voices. I'm with you there, but you don't really give a fuck about the foxes, do you?'

'I do!'

'How come they're still allowed to be killed, only not the same way?'

'We're still campaigning. What matters to us is putting a stop to cruelty as sport.'

'Yeah, and what about this right to roam shit? You want to go where you like, but you don't want bikers doing it. Like I said, you're in it for yourself, just like everyone else, only you don't like to admit it.'

'No. Motorbikes cause far more damage to the environment than walkers, but yes, I do have reservations, and I'm not entirely selfish. I do put the good of the environment in front of my personal needs, and if you're social conscience is so pure, why do you see Tiggy, who stands for just about everything you object to?'

I knew the answer, and so did he: that when it came

to Tiggy, or any other attractive girl, his cock took over from his brain and his principles went straight out of the window. To my surprise he admitted it, more or less.

'Just 'cause she's fit don't mean I have to like what she's into. I like a woman with a bit of fight.'

He looked at me and grinned, his meaning all too obvious. My anger had already been rising and I felt it flare further at his insolence. It would have been hard to miss the irony – when I'd wanted to flirt with him, I ended up arguing and grew even angrier when he made just the sort of pass I loved to fantasise about. At the same instant my stomach gave a familiar jump, and I bit back my instinctive answer, giving him a chance to speak before I could find another.

'What, you going to tell me to piss off now, 'cause I don't fit in your cosy little world?'

There was more than a trace of a sneer in his voice. I could never have done it, not if I hadn't been angry, but as it was the words had tumbled out of my mouth before I could think better of it.

'You're right, yes, I should throw you out, but just to prove that your preconceptions are wrong: do you want to go to bed with me?'

If he ran I'd have turned the tables on him. If he didn't . . .

He just started, all his cocksure male certainty gone in an instant, transformed from a brash, anarchic rebel to an inexperienced lad with a few words. I wasn't even sure he thought my offer was genuine, but his reaction had filled me with confidence. He was still gaping like a fish as I stood up and offered my hand.

'Come on, or you can leave.'

All I got out of him was a faint gurgle, but he taken my hand. I led him towards the door, my heart hammering and the blood singing in my head, but determined not to betray my feelings. Perhaps it wasn't how I'd imagined it would be in my fantasies, but *he* was, every bit as rough and ready, and every bit as male. As we reached the stairs he got over his shock and began to behave like one, letting go of my hand to take me in his arms, kissing me as he began to paw my bottom through my skirt.

I returned his kiss, eager to have him take control and making no effort to stop him or even slow him down as he began to tug my skirt up my thighs. He was eager, his doubt gone, groping clumsily at my body in his urgency to have me, as if he wanted to do everything at once. I had to shrug my own jacket off, but it caught halfway, trapping my arms, and with that I was lost completely. His fingers were on the buttons of my blouse and I couldn't reach to stop him if I wanted to.

My eyes closed, my head went back and he was kissing my neck as he fumbled my buttons wide, tearing one in his eagerness, and a second, before jerking it open across my breasts. Again his arms came around me, fumbling for my bra catch as he kissed at my neck and face and mouth. My bra came loose, he had tugged the cups up and my breasts were bare to his hands, then to his mouth. It hurt a little, too eager as he bit and sucked at my nipples, but I didn't try to stop him. My blouse had fallen from my shoulders, adding to my trapped feeling, and he was fumbling my skirt higher up.

I went down to the pressure of his hands as he pushed, now passive as he sat me on the stairs. As he groped for the top of my tights he was already on top of me, clumsier and more urgent than ever. One jerk and I was bare, my knickers gone too, and he was rolling up my legs, pressing down on me, my body completely open to him, my arms trapped, his fingers fumbling for his fly, something firm and round pressing between my thighs, and inside, pushed deep up with one firm thrust.

He caught onto me, pumping with desperate energy as our mouths met once more in a hard, urgent kiss. I could taste him and smell the leather of his jacket, feel his weight on top of me and the bulk of him inside me, deeper and faster, faster still, to bring me right to the edge of orgasm – as good as I could ever get without my own fingers – and hold me there. He said something, calling me a dirty name between clenched teeth, gripped on tighter still, now pressing right into me with every push, and I was there, gasping with ecstasy, my response as helpless as my body as I came.

So did he, with a final grunt, deep inside before jerking himself free, catching me by my head, pulling my body forward on the stairs and sliding his cock into my mouth. I took it, sucking as best I could as he came down from his climax with a long sigh of satisfaction.

7

I had done it, made love to the sort of man I liked to fantasise about. No, made love was the wrong expression. That was what I did with Robert. With Dean I'd had sex.

That was what I'd wanted, and it was what I'd got. Inevitably my feelings were ambivalent, with measures of irresponsibility and guilt taking something of the glow of satisfaction that was my main reaction. In theory there was no problem at all with Robert. He was as much against the idea that a man could have an exclusive right to a woman as I was, but that was theory, and in practice it might be a very different matter. There was also Tiggy, but as she seemed determined not to be tied down to one man she clearly had no right to be jealous and I had no reason to feel bad. Nevertheless, the sensible thing was not to tell either of them.

I couldn't pretend I liked Dean, and I had no particular intention of doing it again, let alone starting any sort of relationship. What I did with others was an entirely different matter, because after finding the courage to make that all-important first move once, I was sure that it would be a great deal easier the next time. When, and with whom, I didn't know, but I was sure it would happen.

Despite my misgivings I was in a very good mood indeed the following day. I'd achieved two important goals, to break through what had always seemed to be an impenetrable glass ceiling between Keynes and the old established universities and to make fantasy reality. Admittedly in the second case it hadn't been something I'd been aiming at, just the opposite if anything, but my previous thoughts on the matter now seemed rather too black and white. Dean had certainly been rough with me, and once he was sure he had the green light he'd given me very little say in what happened, but the decision to allow that had been mine and mine alone.

It was only after he had left that I began to think of Tiggy again. She hadn't come back by midnight and I was beginning to worry rather more, especially as I'd thought she was with Saul but Dean insisted he was in Norwich. Reading between the lines it seemed likely that he'd come round in the hope of having sex with her while his friend was elsewhere, but in the circumstances that was hardly important. What was important was her safety, and I decided to ring the following morning.

When I did she answered immediately, her voice rather formal for just a moment before changing to her usual breezy confidence. She was in Brancaster, and was so obviously fully in control of what was going on that I ended up making an excuse for ringing, pretending that I was checking she had everything she needed for her essay. Not only did she, but she had finished it.

I was left feeling rather foolish as I cut the connection, but also so sunny it put a self-deprecating smile on my face. After all, she was safe, and that was what mattered. With that last worry gone I was happier than ever, not only feeling that my life was suddenly more exciting, but also more desirable and confident in myself than for a long time. Dean, after all, was used to sex with Tiggy, but he clearly found me physically attractive.

There was a great deal to do, having rearranged my schedule to make time for my visit to Cambridge, and more because I hadn't expected to be signed up immediately and therefore needed to pick up some background on the three theses I would be examining. Paddon sounded easy enough, as his work was so close to my own, but I still needed to get a clear idea of exactly what he was doing. I knew nothing at all about Simmons and Ray, and after an hour in the library when I would normally have been having lunch I could see that I was going to have to put in some work on all three.

Laura Simmons was first and foremost a marine-biologist with interests along similar lines to those of Dr Davis-Brown. Her funding came direct from the Ministry, for analysis of cod fry densities in the North Sea. It was not my area as such, but there was a good deal of overlap in terms of her statistical methods, which was presumably why I'd been chosen. I would need to keep an eye on the relevant journals and back reference, but otherwise it was straightforward.

Anil Ray was funded by the college and to judge from his work he was being groomed to take over from Davis-Brown as an authority on marine crustacea, although there was the inevitable nod towards practicality in his choice of research. Again it would be largely a matter of expanding my reading.

Phil Paddon's work was not dissimilar to what Tiggy was doing for her assignment, although in far broader scope, looking at the effects of human presence on every habitat for which he'd been able to find an adequate amount of existing data, including not only those typical of East Anglia and the Midlands but others as far afield as Wales. He was clearly ambitious, which made me keen to do him justice.

I left the library with a quarter of an hour to spare before my one o'clock lecture, hoping to grab a vegetable samosa on my way, only for Sarah to beckon to me from the registration desk as I passed. Hoping she wasn't going to ask me to cover up some new piece of criminal behaviour for her, I went across. She spoke in an urgent whisper as soon as I reached her.

'You've got the video safe, haven't you?'

'Yes, of course. Robert has made a CD and I have the original tape for back-up.'

'Good. You know the county plod, and this is not going to be easy. We need our evidence absolutely solid.'

'Of course.'

'We'll also need to show the original tape, or there could be accusations of doctoring. For now I'm going to make an appointment with a sympathetic solicitor to discuss our plan of campaign, and we each need to prepare an exact statement, making very sure our stories match and that nothing we did that day could possibly be interpreted as in breach of the law.'

I nodded, not having intended to admit to indecent exposure in any case, never mind whatever other offences Robert and I might have committed. She obviously had more to say, but I was determined to get my lunch and stepped quickly back.

'Leave it with me, Sarah, and I'll make sure Robert knows too.'

Making sure I got something for lunch was only one reason for not talking to Sarah too long. I wanted my weekend free and she was more than likely to want me to help out with some protest or other. No doubt it would be a worthy cause, and no doubt I would end up going, but if I never found out about it she couldn't cajole me into getting involved.

What I wanted to do was go up to the north of the county and look at some of the sites relating to Phil Paddon's work, along with two of those being used by students on second year assignments, in particular Tiggy's. I had faith in her ability and there was no doubt she had put a lot of work in, but as her supervisor I needed to have been over the same ground at the very least. If anything, she had put too much work in. When she had asked if she could miss the occasional lecture I hadn't expected her to spend most of the week away, and I was concerned it would be detrimental to her other work.

I was perfectly within my rights, but I still felt a little awkward about it, as if I was intruding on her personal space, and made worse by the way I'd let her get inside my imagination. Telling myself that I shouldn't allow my private thoughts to interfere with my work was all very well, but it did little to alter the way I felt. The best thing seemed to be to wait until she got back, ask her to point out where she'd been working on a map along with a summary of her research and go up there on my own. Unfortunately she didn't come back. Dean did.

He was at the corner of the Close when I came home, slouched over his motorbike and in the company of two friends, both of whom I recognised as Tiggy's hangers-on. Despite a mild sense of irritation I greeted them with a smile, which Dean returned with a lazy gesture of his hand.

'Hey, Hazel. Coming riding?'

The other two grinned. I kept smiling and pushed out the pile of papers I was carrying, determined to be diplomatic.

'I'd love to, but not this evening. I have to read through these essays.'

'Dump the essays. We'll go for a ride.'

'I really can't. They need to be ready for my tutorials tomorrow and Friday. Another time, if you like?'

'That's cool. See you.'

He repeated the lazy gesture and swung his motorbike around, the others imitating him and all three roaring off up the main road, Dean briefly lifting his bike onto one wheel. I gave a nervous glance to the neighbours' houses and was sure I saw Mrs Tattershal's net curtains twitch, but ignored her as I walked on.

Indoors, I put the essays down on the kitchen table and ate an avocado thoughtfully as I analysed my own reaction. I really hadn't been able to spare the time, but was I also using that as an excuse to avoid what might have happened? There were three of them, and to judge by the grins of the other two Dean had told them about the night before. Perhaps they'd been hoping to share me, perhaps they still did?

It was definitely a thought for later, but work is work. Retiring to the living room, I put my feet up and began to read through the essays, quickly losing myself in the intricacies of the effects of nitrogenous fertilisers on habitat in the Norfolk Broads, or rather, the student's opinions thereof. All of them had read the standard works and reached the standard conclusions, varying only in their analysis of possible remedies. I marked them as conscientiously as was possible given the very similar content, before making myself a snack of pasta and sun-dried tomatoes and pouring a glass of red wine as I pondered how it might have been possible to improve on the answers.

The next morning I found out. Tiggy's essay arrived in the post, and it was a masterpiece. Not only had she considered several species and three locations that had not been included in any of the set texts, but her ideas on solutions to the problem took into account both political and economic factors, concluding that full regeneration was impossible unless the use of fertiliser in the entire watershed dropped by seventy-five per cent. The figure seemed a little more precise than I felt justified, but otherwise her work could not be faulted.

In fact it was so good that I wondered if she might have bought it on the internet, only to almost immediately dismiss the idea. Nobody who had not both read the full spectrum of literature and been on the ground could possibly have known so much, let alone interviewed the managers of two local agricultural combines, which Tiggy apparently had. Evidently she hadn't been wasting her time at all; far from it.

I half expected Dean and his friends to turn up again that evening, but they didn't, nor the next, provoking a mixture of relief and disappointment. Robert and I went out on the Friday to The Artichoke, then back to his flat, where we made love in conventional fashion. He was hoping to make a weekend of it, but I declined his offer, promising to see a play together on the Monday night instead. I could sense his disappointment as I left, leading to a touch of guilt and having to tell myself very firmly that the reason I didn't want him with me over the weekend had nothing to do with the fact that I might be seeing Tiggy.

She still wasn't back on the Saturday morning, so I called her, getting a sleepy answer just as I was about to give up.

'Hello?'

'Tiggy? Hi, this is Hazel. Did I wake you up?'

'Yes, but that's OK. I'm sorry I haven't been ...'

'That's all right, at least for now, although we do need to discuss it. What I called to say is that I'm going to be up in Brancaster today and I'm hoping you'll have time to show me what you've been doing.'

'Brancaster? Um ... sure, no problem. What time? It's just that I have to see somebody in the morning.'

'Lunchtime would be fine, or later?'

'Later. Make it, um ... three?'

'If you like. Whereabouts shall we meet?'

'Um ... the church?'

'If you like. Where are you staying? Or the car park at the front is always easy.'

'The car park at the front. That's good. Three o'clock?'

'Yes. See you there.'

I was smiling to myself as I closed my phone. She'd been half asleep, no doubt after whatever she'd been up to the night before, as to judge by her diary she seemed to need at least some sexual contact every day. Presumably there would be the occasional gap, but if I was right in thinking that what she did, and what she wrote down, related in some way to a catharsis for the rejection of her religion then there was presumably more to it than simply her biological drive.

As I began to drive north I considered the matter, also hoping I might be able to bring it into conversation without giving myself away. Only when I was well outside the town did I put my mind back to what I was supposed to be doing and turn towards Fakenham and the nearest of Phil Paddon's habitat sites. It was a stretch of heathland near Massingham for which records of both fauna and flora went right back to the eighteenth century.

I already knew it fairly well, having been involved in the negotiations to preserve it as a site of scientific interest, which we had only succeeded in doing subject to agreeing to let it be managed as a human resource. Robert and I had been on opposing sides in the debate, and it had been my ability to influence him which prevented it from becoming open access. As it was, the heath was criss-crossed with marked walks but the areas between were undisturbed, at least in theory.

My first impression was that half the population of the UK seemed to have been having their picnics there, not to mention other things. The car park was a disgrace, strewn with litter, including condoms, and the burnt-out wreck of a car. I made a note to write to the appropriate authorities and pushed deeper, along a path between stands of silver birch, broom and gorse.

For the first fifty yards or so I grew increasingly pessimistic. There was less litter, but a maze of small paths running between the bushes and joining areas of flattened grass that had definitely been used for sex and possibly for taking drugs. A good many people also seemed to have been riding both mountain bikes and motorbikes, in some places scuffing the soil down to the chalk beneath.

Only deeper in was the habitat less disturbed, and I'd quickly managed to identify a broad range of typical heathland species, both plant and animal. Having seen the figures, I knew there had been a gradual decline in diversity, particularly among bird species, and I was interested to see if it had continued, a depressing possibility but one that would vindicate my report.

What I did see was a Red Kite, the forked tail unmistakable as it flew in lazy zigzags over a stand of pine to one side of the heath. Just for it to be there was remarkable, so far from the release site in the Chilterns, despite the similar habitat, which went a long way to lifting my spirits. If it was resident, then Phil Paddon would have no doubt noticed it, probably along with several hundred twitchers, and I decided not to report the sighting and risk any influence on his results.

Despite having walked the best part of two miles around the heath I was still going to be early, and stopped off at a pub north of Fakenham, only to discover that not a single item on their menu was vegetarian. Burnham Market proved more fruitful and I sat on the green to eat, and to glance at my watch with increasing impatience. Even after I had finished eating I was half-an-hour early at Brancaster, but drove down to the car park anyway.

It was much as I remembered it, with the peculiar gate to the golf course, the club house and mile upon mile of dunes and sand. There was no sign of Tiggy, but I didn't need her to see that it was an ideal place, with the levels of human disturbance and erosion easily quantified, so much so the whole area might have been from a diagram in a book rather than real. Given that, Tiggy wasn't a local, which suggested she had put in a lot of careful research before making her decision.

I had climbed to the top of one of the dunes when I saw her arrive, on the back of a motorbike driven by a man in black leathers. They kissed when she dismounted. They were too far away for me to see his face as he lifted his helmet, but I was certain he could only be Saul, whatever Dean had said. Evidently something was going on, but it was probably a simple matter of rivalry among the bikers and none of my business in any case.

By the time I had walked around to the car park he was gone and Tiggy was brushing out her hair at the side of the road. She smiled and waved as she saw me, starting forward immediately as she dug a sheaf of notes from the rucksack she had already taken from her back.

'Hello, Dr Jones ... Hazel, sorry, I can never get used to that.'

I wanted to ask about Saul, but it was plainly inappropriate and I simply returned her greeting instead, taking the notes as she offered them. There was plenty of it, mostly photocopies of the same basic map, but illustrated with distribution charts for a range of species, schematic diagrams to show the effects of winds, currents, longshore drift, tidal maxima and minima, charts to show erosion, pollution and microhabitat, even a series of historical comparisons. Tiggy gave a faint shrug as I reached the end.

'That's as far as I've got, I'm afraid.'

'No, this is extraordinary work. I can see you haven't been wasting your time, but really, it's far more than you need. Please don't take this the wrong way, because I'm very impressed, especially as your essay was by far the best this week, but I'm not at all sure you'll have time to write this up properly.'

'Don't you think so?'

'No. It has to be in by the end of term, after all, and statistical analysis alone will be a major project. To get even an approximate idea of the influence of each of these factors you will need to do a full scale multiple-regression, while all I really need is to know that you've taken them into account.'

'Oh.'

'It's not that I doubt you're ability, Tiggy, only that you will be able to find the time. Have you done anything in the way of statistics? Beyond the basic first year course, that is.'

'No.'

'In that case I recommend limiting the scope of your project to working out a correlation between the effects of human pressure on the environment and biodiversity. That will be more than adequate. Even at a glance I imagine you'll get a significant result, and you should be able to show cause and effect.'

She nodded, rather shy for her.

'OK. I'll do that.'

'Good. Shall we walk up and down the beach?'

'Sure.'

It had occurred to me that she might have simply photocopied the maps and added the data to create plausible results, hardly a worthy thought, but it wouldn't have been the first time. Yet as she guided me first west to the nature reserve and then east again to the limit of the golf course it quickly grew plain that not only was her data accurate, but that she had recorded it with great care.

By the time we turned back at the far end of the golf course I was fully content in her ability. We'd not only discussed her assignment, but her essay and other work, and, while unsurprisingly she had missed quite a lot from those lectures she'd failed to attend, she seemed to have made up for it in other areas. Nevertheless, she had exams to take, and exams meant concentrating on the course, so as we walked back along the sand with the sun dipping slowly towards the horizon in front of us I found myself giving advice.

'You've been doing some exceptional work, Tiggy, but I am concerned by the amount of time you've been putting into it. The way the examination system works, you do need to concentrate first and foremost on the syllabus, and I'm concerned that you haven't been doing that.'

'I know, you're right. I promise I'll do better.'

'It's not so much a question of doing better, but of priorities.'

'I understand, and I think I've done just about everything I can here anyway.'

'You've done far more than you needed to, but please don't think of what I'm saying as criticism. If you do choose to go on and try for an MSc or a doctorate your enthusiasm will count for a great deal.'

She nodded but didn't answer, her expression thoughtful as she walked on in silence. We were the only people on the beach, the footsteps we'd made going in the opposite direction the only human ones marking the sand left smooth by the retreating tide. Tiggy was barefoot, her boots and socks in her hands and her jeans rolled up, and had begun to walk in her own steps, a carefree, almost childish gesture I found immensely appealing, and all the more so for her beautiful yet serious face and the way her long hair moved in the gentle breeze.

For one moment the urge to explain everything to her was almost overpowering. I even opened my mouth, at the very least intending to say that the house had seemed lonely without her, only to change my mind, sure that the comment would give away those feelings I was trying so hard to suppress at that moment and spoil the very pleasant if rather academic friendship we had built up. Instead I stayed silent, contenting myself with simply walking beside her, full of regret.

I also felt a good degree of self-deprecation, both bitter and humorous. How could I possibly be falling for Tiggy? It was such a ridiculously foolish thing to do, and just the sort of thing I had always looked on with so much contempt in men. I was thirty-five, an at least moderately successful academic with my life as I wanted it and, as any therapist would have pointed out immediately, for me to yearn after a younger man, or in this case a younger woman, had very little to do with love or even lust, and a great deal to do with my wanting to sublimate my own needs for hers. The same applied even to reading her diary.

Yet I knew that if I stayed in Brancaster with her the chances of my saying or even doing something inappropriate were all too real. It was bad enough at Keynes, but by the sea, after a meal and wine, it might be too much. Also, she undoubtedly had plans of her own, and could do without me hanging around. After all, there was a huge difference between the Tiggy of my fevered imagination and the bright, socially skilled young woman I had spent the afternoon with.

Despite that, as I drove east after leaving her in the hope of finding a reasonable hotel in Wells, I couldn't help but speculate as to whether it might just have been possible to make fantasy reality. After all, it had worked with Dean, after only a moment of boldness, and Tiggy was undoubtedly sexually attracted to women. If Janice, then why not me? She seemed remarkably open in her choices, and if not me, then might it not work as I wanted it to?

Unfortunately the answer was clear. I could accept that there was a measure of latent lesbianism within me. I could accept my desire to take a sexually submissive role. I could accept the social implications of living with another woman, and one so much younger than myself. What I could never accept was a relationship with one of my own students, which was not only unethical, but illegal.

8

It was really just as well, because even allowing for my ability to cope with the implications of what I wanted, there were far too many ifs and buts to have ever made it work. Not least was Tiggy's own attitude; as while I knew she was bisexual I had no reason to think she was interested in me. Even if she had been there was the question of coping with my desire to be bound and controlled by her, which if anything seemed to run in parallel with her own desires rather than in a complementary opposition.

I was thinking about it for most of the following day as I drove from site to site across along the north and east coasts of Norfolk and back across the Broads towards Keynes. The situation was clearly hopeless, and the more I thought about it the more annoyed I grew with my reactions and my inability to control them. Yet by the time I got home I had decided on a rational course of action and was determined to follow it, putting my emotional needs firmly in second place. I had a perfectly good relationship with Robert, and that was what I should be working on, not yearning after an impossibly inappropriate relationship with Tiggy Blackmore, nor messing about with motorbike yobs from the Cornridge Estate.

Yes, I could indulge my penchant for having my hands tied, but only within the confines of a safe, mature relationship. Perhaps I would even introduce some of my other fantasy ideas into the relationship, just to give it new life, but that would be all. That *would* be all. No young men. No women. No group sex. No risky exhibitionism.

As I'd arranged to see Robert on the Monday evening anyway, that was clearly the ideal time to make a new start. I hadn't treated him very well, I could see, taking advantage of his patience and his determination not to behave in a stereotypically male fashion. Now I would make up for it, taking him to The Artichoke before the play, and offering whatever sexual pleasure took his fancy afterwards.

Eve had recommended the play – an adaptation of *Beowulf* set within the Glaswegian drinking culture at the student union – which she said was both clever and funny. Robert had his doubts about the social messages it appeared to send, both in terms of alcoholism and violence, to say nothing of the implied ridicule of the working class, but I'd already managed to persuade him to go and see it before making a judgement.

As it turned out it was extremely funny, and also thought-provoking, although it was impossible to deny that Robert had at least some grounds for his reservations. Personally, after sharing a bottle of wine at The Artichoke, I was feeling sufficiently mellow to enjoy it and leave the questions until later, while the appearance of Grendel's mother as a gigantic washerwoman clutching a bottle of tonic wine in one hand had me laughing out loud.

By the time it finished I was in just the right mood to make my offer to Robert; well fed but not too much, pleasantly tipsy and happy with laughing. As we left the union building we were in the thick of the crowd, hardly the place for that sort of conversation, and Robert was doing his best to come to terms with his enjoyment of the play.

'... at a gut level, yes, I admit it was quite funny, but I do feel they might have chosen a more suitable topic for their satire.'

'How could they? Surely it was Glaswegian drinking culture they'd chosen to parody using *Beowulf* as a medium rather than the reverse?'

'That's true, yes, but why chose that to parody in the first place? Why not ... I don't know, American militarism, or the situation in the EU?'

'For one thing both of those are already widely parodied. At least this was original, and daring.'

'Why daring?'

'Because it does challenge our perceptions of what's acceptable within society and what isn't. Besides, I suspect the principle motive force behind it was comedy rather than social comment, and you have to admit that it worked.'

'True ...'

He trailed off, although I could tell that his conscience was still pricking him. We'd reached the car park, moving away from the main body of students and with those who'd driven now seeking out their vehicles. That seemed to be everyone except us, and as we reached the road we were alone. I felt wonderfully relaxed, in no great hurry, but looking forward to whatever the evening might bring. Only when we'd gone far enough for the traffic noise not to matter did I speak.

'I'm sorry if I was a bit short with you after the sabbing the other day.'

'That's all right, don't mention it.'

'No, really. After all, it was entirely my fault, and you did the right thing.'

I took his hand and smiled as he looked around.

'It was nice too, I mean, what we were doing before

the hunt arrived, really nice. I'd like to do it again, sometime, but not this evening. This evening I'd like to return the favour.'

He looked worried.

'You want to tie me up?'

I laughed.

'No! That's not what I meant, unless that's what you'd like. What I mean is, I'll do anything you like, anything at all. Just name it.'

To my surprise his expression grew more worried still.

'I don't know if I could do that.'

'Why not?'

'I just couldn't. I'd feel I was exploiting you.'

'Exploiting me? Don't be silly! I want you to, or I wouldn't have asked.'

'Yes, but still. It wouldn't really be what you wanted, would it?'

'Maybe ... maybe not, but it would probably be fun, and if it's too outrageous I'll tell you. Come on, Robert, tell me, and be adventurous. After all, I might not know if I like it or not until I've tried it.'

'I'm sorry, but I could never do that to a woman. It would still feel like exploitation.'

I wanted to laugh, but he looked deadly serious and I held back, not sure what I could say. His argument was one I'd heard before, many a time, but always applied to situations in which for social or economic reasons, even fear, the woman had to do as she was told or accept consequences. That hardly applied to our relationship. To suggest it did was insulting, and that did need to be said.

'Robert, this is me, Hazel, and I have just made you an offer most men would jump at, of my own free will and because I actively want you to do it. You can be very sure that if you chose anything I consider unacceptable I will say so, not that I suppose you will for a moment, and I assure you that you will not be exploiting me!'

He hesitated, caught between opposing principles of socially acceptable thought: the need to accommodate me sexually as a woman and the need not to be exploitative in his behaviour. I waited, allowing him to take his time as we walked on, sure there would be something lurking in the deepest part of his mind, something he had never dared admit to me, but which would provide me the same sort of sudden sharp arousal I'd experienced with Dean, or thinking about Tiggy. When he did speak it wasn't at all what I'd expected.

'Is this because you feel our relationship is going downhill?'

'No! Not at all, I just –'

'Wanted to add some spice to our sex life? I've read the books too, Hazel.'

He sounded hurt and accusing, as if what I'd asked was tantamount to a threat to leave him unless he complied. Again I laughed, although it was a trifle forced.

'Don't be silly, Robert! I just want to say thank you, that's all. It took a lot of courage for me to ask what I did, and you were really good about it, so I'd like to return the favour. That's it, no hidden agenda, no conditions, no consequences.'

Again he went quiet and my hopes rose, imaging him plucking up the courage to bring some little gem of naughtiness up from his carefully suppressed darker side. Finally he spoke.

'I . . . I'm really very content the way things are.'

'Oh. It's nice of you to say that, of course, but there

must be some facet of your sexuality you'd like to explore, surely?'

'I like pleasing you.'

'Fine, that's nice, but maybe in some special way?'

'I can't think of anything, and of course female sexuality is so much more complex than male, so . . .'

'That old chestnut won't wash, Robert. You know perfectly well it's only the result of peer pressure and general social conditioning. After all, a lot of people would consider what you do like as unconventional, even immoral, and definitely less than fully masculine.'

'I'd like to think I'm beyond that stage.'

'You are, absolutely, and I appreciate that. Would you like to take the idea further?'

'How do you mean?'

'I don't know, you should be telling me! Maybe . . . maybe as you like to go down for me a little role play would make it stronger. Tell me, Robert. Do you like to cross dress, maybe? I imagine you could just about get a pair of my knickers on.'

'No, really, I'm fine the way we are.'

'OK, but you can say, I won't mind, anything. Maybe you'd like me to give you a good spanking? I could even dress up in that army gear we used –'

'Hazel!'

'Not that. How about doing it to me, then?'

'I couldn't possibly!'

'No, I don't suppose you could, but there must be something, surely? Do you feel any need for male interaction, perhaps to take another man in your mouth while I watch? I'd like that.'

If I'd thought he'd looked worried before I hadn't known what the word meant.

'Is . . . is that what you want me to do, have it with another man?'

'Not necessarily, no! Not unless you want to.'

'No! Not that I have anything against gay men, not in the least, or lesbians either, or any valid sexual orientation. I'm not homophobic, but I have no personal...'

'OK, something else, then. Come on, Robert, I'm trying really hard here, and you're not helping. There must be something!'

He shrugged, looking deeply uncomfortable as we walked on. I was beginning to get annoyed, despite also turning myself on with what I was saying, especially the idea of having him go down for another man. We'd been heading for his flat by unspoken agreement. I knew he would want to make love and, given what I was offering him, I couldn't see why he had to make life difficult. At the least he could have asked some minor favour, something we didn't usually do. I was waiting for him to sort himself out, and he didn't speak until we were almost there.

'Hazel, I really think you ... we, should speak to a counsellor, maybe a therapist too.'

I stopped dead in my tracks.

'Why?'

'Why? Isn't that obvious? You're not happy with the way things are between us, and aside from that I'm worried about you ... you know, wanting your hands tied and ... and the things you've been saying! I ...'

'What? Robert, I do not need to see a counsellor, and I certainly do not need to see a therapist! For goodness sake, it was just a game, just fun!'

'Yes, darling, but I'm concerned for your underlying motives.'

'Which you feel a therapist would be able to under-stand better than I do myself? I do know my own mind, Robert, and I assure you that I am quite capable of managing my own sexuality!'

'What I'm trying to say, Hazel –'

'Is that I'm mentally ill, just because I want to put a bit of fun into our sex life? For goodness sake try and get things in perspective!'

'No, seriously, Hazel, you know I respect your intelligence, but I think you're blind to your own –'

'No, Robert, I am not. I am fully in touch with my own sexuality, believe me, and I might have hoped that you would have supported me in seeking to develop that. Why do you have to be so bloody correct?'

'Correct?'

'Yes, correct. What happened to trying to extend your tolerance beyond conventional boundaries? It's not even as if I've been with a bloody goat, either!'

'Hazel, you're getting upset now.'

'Yes, I am. Just go home, Robert!'

I turned on my heel, seething with anger, both for his attitude and the whole fabric of what was and what was not acceptable. It was bad enough with the play, when you weren't even supposed to laugh at something because the humour drew on an unfortunate situation, let alone the assumption that any sexual activity beyond the narrow confines of current thinking needed the attentions of a therapist. As I walked back towards the High Street I wanted to scream.

Robert hadn't even followed me, but stayed on the corner looking like a sorrowful sheep. I didn't care, unable to bear his company for another moment, feeling insulted, and even more, unappreciated. Any man should have been grateful, or at the very least intrigued, and as my anger began to cool I could already feel the hurt to my confidence. That, and the sure knowledge that I'd now spend a lonely, restless night questioning my own choices brought my blood back to the boil.

I needed a drink, and I wasn't even going to feel guilty about the number of units of alcohol involved. In fact I needed more than that. I needed everything that broke the rules, a whole bottle of strong red wine to wash down a huge, meaty steak, like the sort my Dad had always cooked and which I'd loved so much before I developed my wretched conscience. I needed a car too, and not my squeaky little box on wheels, but a great roaring, guzzling monster with a six-litre engine and the carbon dioxide emission levels of a small country. I needed a man, and not some whinging specimen in touch with his feminine side but a great big, red-bloodied, stiff-cocked male, someone who'd take me and fuck me – yes, that was the right word – and make a real pig of himself with my body.

That I could do. A little way down the street a take-away was still open, creating an arc of bright yellow light on the pavement and the edge of the road, where three motorbikes were propped, their riders lounging nearby, holding big greasy burgers and drinking from cans of lager – Dean and two of his friends. I didn't even slow down, knowing full well that common sense would get the better of me if I hesitated for a moment, but walked straight up to them.

'Is that offer of a ride still open?'

Dean's back was to me, and he almost choked on his burger as I spoke. Both his friends were already looking at me and grinning before he managed to turn round and focus on who it was.

'Hazel? Hi ... yeah, yeah.'

He was mumbling as he tried to cram the rest of his

burger into his mouth, making his friends laugh, and more as he desperately tried to recover his cool. I'd crossed my arms and stood waiting, my heart already hammering in my chest.

'You want a ride, let's go. See you, boys.'

'Who says they don't get to come?'

I'd said it before I'd even begun to engage my brain, and then it was too late. Dean looked surprised, but only for a moment, and both the others gave gleeful whoops and scrambled for their bikes, one not even bothering to finish his burger. Both had started their machines before Dean had even mounted up, and were revving their engines as I climbed on the back. I had no helmet, I was in a skirt and a cotton blouse, but I didn't care. The thrill as we tore down the High Street with my hair blowing free and the wind cool in my face blended with my anger at Robert to bring me to a natural high better than anything but sex, and it seemed more than likely I'd be getting that too, and soon.

Robert had decided to follow after all, and as we passed I gave a cheerful wave, leaving him standing gaping in the street, lost to view as we turned north. I clung on tight, my arms around Dean's lean, hard body, revelling in what I was doing and absolutely determined to ignore the nagging voice of my better judgement. Not that I had much choice, the sound of the engine too loud to speak to Dean and the bike going far too fast for me to think of getting off.

I had no idea where we were going, but they seemed to, out on the Fakenham Road, faster and faster still as the traffic cleared, until we were beyond the lights, with only our own beams to cut the darkness. Already I felt as if I was in a dream, riding through the night with a man little more than half my age and his two companions on a promise of rough, uninhibited sex. It was just the sort of thing Tiggy might have done, had done many a time, no doubt, and now it was my turn.

It wasn't until we arrived that I realised where we were, on the heathland near Massingham, the same car park I'd stopped in only two days before. That seemed an age ago and a world away, the black loom of the trees against the sky and the shadows thrown among the gorse and broom by our headlights now creating a place at once frightening and promising; a place where I could let myself go, completely.

The moment we stopped I climbed off, my legs shaking, my body trembling with adrenaline from the ride and the prospect of what was to come. As the bike engines muttered down to silence and the lights died away I was left blinking in absolute darkness, fading only slightly as my eyes adjusted to the moonlight, with the three men now dark shapes among others. Dean spoke first.

'What's up, babe?'

Suddenly I didn't know what to do, or what to say. I'd assumed they would, but there was uncertainty in his voice, and I answered quickly, not wanting to spoil the moment.

'Whatever you like.'

Whatever I like, huh?'

There was laughter in his voice, a touch mocking, and his words were addressed to his friends as much as to me. I realised that if anything was to happen, or at least anything beyond simply having sex with Dean while his friends hung back full of jealousy and frustration, then I would have to take control, just as Tiggy did. As I answered him it was the sound of my voice, but it sounded strange in my ears.

'Uh, uh, let's play fair boys. Come with me.'

I knew where to go, roughly, and they seemed to as well, in among the shadows of the bushes to the nearest of the grassy areas. Twice cars had passed on the road, and whatever I was going to do I did not intend it to be a public performance. My heart was beating furiously, the little voice of my common sense now screaming at me to stop, to run as far away as I could, but I was determined to follow my desire. Dean and one of his friends remained silent, the other giggled nervously as I got down, squatting on the dew-soaked grass.

All I could see were shadows, but I could feel, the texture of denim and leather, the folds of their flies and the metal of their zips. One of them swore as I peeled his zip down. Dean told him to shut up and then swore himself as my hand burrowed into the front of his fly, to pull down his boxers and take his cock in my hand. As the feel and scent of him caught me the last of my reservation dissolved. I took him in, sucking eagerly as I groped for the others.

One hand was taken and guided to a smooth, firm erection, the other I pulled out myself and I was doing it, pleasuring three men at once as I squatted down on the darkened heath – an act so gloriously inappropriate, so wonderfully arousing, that I already wanted to come. I could just imagine what all my friends would think, how they'd whisper together in mock sympathy and a disapproval very real but tinged with jealousy. How they'd say I was going through some sort of crisis and that I needed help, how it was such a shame.

It wasn't a shame at all; it was great, so rude, and so free. All of them were now erect, what shyness they'd had gone in the security of the darkness and the excitement of the moment. I slowed down, deliberately, not wanting it to end too soon, and began to share my favours more evenly, taking turns with each of them in my mouth, until my senses were swimming with the scent and taste of man and I needed to come so badly I could no longer hold back. I knew how too, the way I'd so often imagined myself, on all fours as two or more men shared me, and I wasn't going to miss out. When I spoke it was a command.

'Take me, now, my way.'

This time they didn't hesitate. No sooner was I down on all fours than Dean was behind me, scrabbling at my skirt as the others swore and shoved at each other for the privilege of my mouth. I nuzzled my face against the closest and took him in, solving the argument. As I begun to suck once more Dean was busy behind me, my skirt already up, the night air cool on my bare flesh as my tights and knickers were jerked down as one, and his cock pushed deep inside me, all the way.

I was in heaven as they began to fuck me, and there really was no other word for it, their cocks as deep as they would go, my body rocking back and forth between them, my excitement rising high and higher still. Never had I imagined I could be so rude, and for once in my life I didn't need a fantasy to bring myself up towards climax. I had my fantasy right there, just exactly what I needed, taken by two strong young men and fucked and fucked and fucked . . .

Everything came together at once, in my body and in my head. I didn't even touch myself, the feel of them inside me and the motion of my body enough to tip me over the edge, and as I came, so did they, both Dean and his friend, who had immediately been replaced by the third, so that as I came slowly down from my orgasm I still had a beautiful long cock to play with. I didn't know his name or anything about him, and yet

I treated him in a way I had never done for Robert, using my mouth and lips and tongue. He had his trousers down by then, allowing me to pleasure not just his cock, but also his balls, and lower, where his hard, muscular buttocks came together, something I had never, ever, imagined I could do.

Yet I did, and as I licked and kissed I had begun to play with myself again, running through what I'd done over and over in my head and delighting in the way I was serving him. Even when he came I didn't stop, still holding his balls in my mouth and his cock in my hand as I brought myself to a second orgasm yet more intense than the first.

9

What had I done? What I had done was what I should have done years before, stopped worrying about the world for a moment, what I ought to be doing and what other people thought, and just for once really indulge myself.

It still took a bit of coming to terms with, but just the memory of that night kept me happy for the rest of the week. My sole regret was that I didn't have anyone to talk to about it, although it was very tempting indeed to open up to Tiggy, who was finally back and as busy as ever. Despite that, just thinking about it was enough to fill every blank moment, and even those aspects I might easily have seen as negative couldn't bring me down.

For one thing, I was fairly sure that Dean at least had intended to leave me there. By the time I'd finished with the third of them, who I now knew was called Rick, both Dean and the second, Steve, had already started up their bikes. The experience had left me dizzy, faint with effort and with reaction, and they could easily have driven away, but didn't, and from what I'd caught of their whispered conversation it seemed that Rick had talked them out of it.

Yet even that didn't bother me. In fact I found the idea of having to please all three of them and simply being abandoned in the middle of nowhere highly arousing, in theory if not in practice, and that was what I came over as I lay in bed thinking about it the following night. Fantasy aside, I also promised myself to be a little more cautious if anything of the sort happened again.

I wasn't particularly concerned about Robert either, which I'd expected to be. He hadn't left a message, and made no attempt to get in contact over the next few days, so I assumed he was simply stewing in his own juice and left it at that. Rather than the sense of loss I might have expected, not having him around was rather refreshing and, given what had happened, I felt entirely justified in letting him come to me, or not.

Everything else seemed to be going well too. On the Thursday morning I received a letter stamped with the Merton College crest, from Dr Davis-Brown, to confirm that I would be external examiner for all three PhD students and implying that there was likely to be more work for me in the future. His tone was remarkably friendly, and he even took the trouble to draw my attention to an oil exploration company who were looking for a spokesperson on environmental issues. I went as far as to look it up, and was taken aback by the salary they were offering, but while I might have compromised my principles to some extent, I was not prepared to go that far. Their reputation for riding roughshod over environmental issues was the worst in Northern Europe.

The assignments were also coming together, with both my students and Dr Woolmer's all producing at least competent work and Tiggy's truly exceptional. She had also taken my advice, and spent most of her evenings in, crunching statistics on her computer. Only on the Friday did she allow herself to be lured out by Saul, and even then she was back before midnight, with a look on her face that had me smiling and blushing at the same time.

'I hear you went riding with some of the boys?'

Her tone was friendly, familiar and also rather surprised, making me wonder just how much she knew and setting my cheeks even hotter. It was hard to know what to say in reply, and all my ambivalent feelings for her had come back in a rush as she went on.

'I didn't know you were into that sort of thing at all.'

I wasn't sure if she meant motorbikes or group sex, so I answered as vaguely and as casually as I could manage.

'Oh, I like all sorts of things you might not expect.'

'Such as?'

She sounded as if she was actively teasing me, and as I tried to find an answer I realised that there was still a great deal of inequality in our relationship as tutor and student, and I really owed it both to her and to myself to keep things from getting out of hand. Fortunately she didn't seem to expect an answer, or at least not immediately, and had gone through into the kitchen. I waited as she poured herself a glass of water, trying to think of a sensible response and wanting to tell her everything in detail before offering her the same favour. Her voice floated back to me.

'Would you like to share a bottle of wine?'

Even as she spoke two paths of possibility opened up in front of me. I could accept, and as we drank my defences would begin to slip, as would hers. Eventually I would tell her what had happened on the heath, in detail, and maybe end up saying something very foolish indeed. Whatever her response, the consequences would be disastrous. Or else I could refuse.

'I'd love to, Tiggy, but it's late and I have a lot to do in the morning.'

* * *

Sunday morning was relaxing, but I had a sneaking suspicion it would be the calm before the storm. I knew Robert and I knew he'd have to talk to somebody. No doubt it would be in confidence, but what he said to Paul or Eve was sure to be passed on, and by now it was more than likely that the whole of our set knew not only that he and I had had an argument, but what about, and that I'd been seen riding off into the night on the back of a motorbike. I could even imagine the sort of conversations they'd be having, concerned, well meaning, but ultimately critical. Eventually, after a great deal of discussion, one of them would come and 'talk to me'.

By midday I was guessing who it would be and calculating the probability of each according to who Robert was most likely to have spoken to and how easily they in turn would feel it was their duty to speak to me. There were three main possibilities, Sarah, Paul and Eve. If Sarah knew it would be at second hand, and her attitude was sure to be ambivalent, so she seemed unlikely. Paul would certainly know but would find it awkward speaking to me about it, so was even less likely. Eve was relatively shy, and very much a peace-maker, but the others would probably talk her into it. I'd barely reached my conclusion when the doorbell rang. As I was making my bed I simply called out of the window.

'Hi, Eve. I'll be with you in a moment.'

'Er . . . hi, Hazel. How did you know it was me?'

I didn't bother to answer, but came downstairs. Tiggy was in her room, chewing on the end of a pencil as she poured over her maps of Brancaster Dunes, which were making her think hard, for once. Her diary was on her desk too, open, and the thought of what it contained added to my resolve as I came to the door.

'Come in, Eve. Coffee?'

'That would be nice, thank you.'

She followed me through to the kitchen as I wondered what excuse she'd have found for coming over.

'I wanted to ask you your opinion about the A140 extension.'

'You know that. It will take up less than five per cent of the greenfield area earmarked for housing in the same district. Besides that, from an ecological point of view the banks not only provide what is effectively a protected habitat but will act as an urban corridor for many plant and invertebrate species.'

'So you're in favour of it?'

'No, I'm against it, at least in principle, but we have to get these things in perspective. The land it will replace is likely to be built over anyway, and the great majority is currently agricultural land with minimal species diversity and high use of pesticides and fertilisers. Even the figures for increasing vehicle pollution are debatable, because they don't take into account the corresponding reduction due to changes in central Norwich.'

'Oh.'

'In my ideal world the entire area in question would be given over to wetland and heath, but as it's currently agricultural land that's not going to happen. The best I could hope for would be environmentally friendly farming, but if the land is earmarked for housing, then we need the road as well. The focus of our protest should be against the housing developments.'

'Robert's not going to like that.'

I merely shrugged and put her coffee down on the table. Now she had her opening she would hopefully get to the point.

'Speaking of Robert. What did happen between you two? If you don't mind me asking, that is?'

'I don't mind at all. We got into a silly argument, that's all.'

'Oh ... it's just ... please don't take this the wrong way, Hazel, but he's really rather worried about you. He said you were ... were going through a life crisis, and, well, I wondered if you'd like to talk?'

I took a sip of coffee to allow myself a pause for thought. There were issues I'd have liked to talk over, even though I felt I had it all under control, and it would have been easy to open out to her. It would also have meant my most private affairs being spread all over Keynes in a matter of hours, although by the sound of things that had happened already, at least in part. As I considered how to reply I was earnestly wishing I'd never asked Robert to put me in bondage, but there was also a measure of anger for why I should have to repress my desires among people every one of whom would have claimed to be tolerant of sexual choices. Eve went on before I could decide what to say.

'I understand if you don't, but whatever happens, I'd just like you to know that I'll always be there for support if you need it.'

'Thank you, Eve, I appreciate that, but I'm really quite OK.'

She didn't reply. I could guess what she wanted to ask. Sarah would have come straight out with it. Not Eve. I was going to have to explain, at least in part, but I was not going to make the mistake of admitting to something if there was even the tiniest possibility that Robert hadn't told her.

'What exactly has Robert told you, Eve?'

Her face instantly went pink, as if I'd flicked a switch.

'Um ... just that you'd had a row, and he was a bit worried about some of the things you'd said, you know, in the heat of the moment.'

'Like what? Tell me.'

Pink changed to scarlet.

'That ... that you felt your relationship was getting stale and wanted to spice it up a bit, you know.'

'No I don't. What did he actually say I wanted?'

Scarlet changed to tomato red.

'To ... to do things to each other ... to ...'

'What!?'

Tomato red changed to crimson.

'To ... to role-play domestic violence and sexual abuse, that's what he said.'

'To role-play domestic violence and sexual abuse! He did, did he? The bastard, the little shit!'

Suddenly I was on the verge of tears, but if Robert had been there he'd have learnt all about domestic violence in double-quick time. Eve looked worried and she was stammering as she replied.

'Did ... didn't you?'

My anger was simply too hot to hold myself back.

'No, I did not! I'll tell you what I did, exactly. I offered to do whatever he wanted, sexually, because I wanted to return a special favour, and when he was being a bit shy about it I made a few suggestions. That's what triggered the argument, because he suggested I needed to see a therapist!'

'He said that, but he said it was because you said you liked to be tied up.'

Her face was beetroot red, her eyes wide. I took a deep breath before speaking again, really fighting for control.

'That's true, yes, but it's just something I happen to like. It's not a problem, but a valid expression of my sexuality. It is not something I need to see a therapist about, but it is something very private, and which fucking Robert should not be broadcasting around the entire campus!'

'Sorry, Hazel, I . . .'

'Don't be, Eve. I don't mean to take it out on you. It's not your fault at all, but you can tell Robert from me that if he genuinely had even the slightest bit of the respect for women that he's always going on about, then he shouldn't be discussing my most intimate behaviour.'

She gave me a wan smile. I sat down, suddenly feeling completely drained, but there was more.

'Did he say anything about me going off on the back of a motorbike?'

'Yes, he said you didn't have a helmet on.'

I nearly laughed. It was so like Robert, more concerned that I hadn't followed safety procedure than for what I might have been doing with three bikers. Eve reached a hand out across the table.

'Are you OK, Hazel, really?'

'Yes, I'm fine, or I would be if it wasn't for Robert. Don't worry about me, please.'

She still had her hand stretched out and her face was full of concern. I could see she wanted to say more but wasn't sure how to phrase her questions without offending me. Taking her hand, I went on, knowing that if I didn't defend myself all sorts of assumptions would be made.

'I really do mean it, Eve, there's nothing to worry about. There are no skeletons in the cupboard, no dark secrets from my childhood. It's simply a reaction to constantly having to take decisions, to always being the one people look to for a solution. Because of that it's nice to surrender my control now and then, in a sexual context. In practical terms that relates to having my hands tied. That's all, nothing dangerous, nothing sinister, and, above all, nothing even remotely abusive!'

I would have continued, but didn't, deciding that the bit about wanting to surrender to the sort of people she and I had so often found ourselves in opposition to in real life would be a step too far. In any case she now looked a good deal less doubtful. I gave her hand a squeeze.

'OK?'

She pursed her lips and nodded.

'I can understand that, I think.'

'Good. Can we leave it there, then? What I really don't want is everybody making a huge fuss. I'd rather just get on with life.'

'I respect that. What about Robert?'

'What about him?'

'Just that he's very worried about you, and he doesn't know how you stand.'

'Let's put it this way. If he'd come round and apologised ... no, not even apologised, not necessarily. If he'd come round and tried to talk it over instead of making these awful assumptions about me, then I'd have been quite happy to try and sort things out between us. As it is, I really don't think there's much point, not unless he's prepared to make some major changes in his attitude. I know that sounds really harsh, but if he's not prepared to accept me the way I am, then what's the point?'

She nodded and bit her lip but didn't reply. Short of a miracle, I could see that it really was the end between Robert and me, and there was a lump in my throat, but I was also telling myself I'd made the right decision. Eve squeezed my hand and let go, sitting back as she once more picked up her coffee cup. A gentle tap on the kitchen door attracted my attention and I turned to see Tiggy, looking rather hesitant.

'Sorry, Hazel, I don't mean to interrupt, but might I just go to the fridge?'

'Of course, come in. You're not interrupting at all. Coffee?'

I couldn't help but wonder how much she'd heard.

I spent the rest of Sunday in anticipation of awkward phone calls, none of which materialised. Despite a determination not to behave like a love-sick teenager it was difficult not to feel hurt, or to want Robert to be running after me just so that I could reject him. To keep my mind off things I buried myself in work, first catching up on all the irritating little bits of household paperwork I usually put off to the last possible minute and then writing letters to various authorities to get my point of view across on a whole series of matters.

Monday was much the same, expecting to find Robert waiting for me when I came out of lectures and jumping every time anyone knocked at my door. I couldn't stop thinking about the situation either, and only when the departmental post was brought around did I find anything else to occupy my mind. There was a letter with the distinctive Merton crest on it, which I opened with a sinking feeling, knowing that Dr Davis-Brown had no reason to communicate again so quickly and sure it would be bad news.

It wasn't, just an invitation to dine with him at the college for the coming Friday. I was a little surprised and it was rather short notice, but I could see no reason to refuse. He could hardly be making a play for me, after all, not at his age, and if he had been he presumably wouldn't have invited me to dine in the college hall.

I'd no sooner replied than I realised that I had nothing even remotely appropriate to wear for a formal dinner at a Cambridge College. Technically I knew I should hold myself aloof from anything that smacked of the establishment as much as putting on a frock to dine with a septuagenarian don, but to turn up in jeans and a T-shirt would have only felt foolish. Besides, after what had happened with Robert I was in no mood for gestures of anti-establishment solidarity, but I was in the mood for treating myself to a dress.

With my last lecture at two o'clock I had plenty of time to go into town afterwards and, despite a slight tendency to glance over my shoulder, I was feeling pretty good. An hour and a half later I wasn't, having been round all three stores and not found anything I could bear to be seen in. Not that there wasn't plenty of choice, but everything either seemed to have been made by sweated labour in the Third World, contain man-made fibres or be hideously expensive, and even then nothing seemed to fit in with the atmosphere of gothic gravitas I'd picked up in Merton.

I came out of Foxes feeling more than a little fed up and wondering if Dr Davis-Brown would regard me as charmingly eccentric or just plain batty if I went in men's black-tie instead, of which there seemed to be plenty at relatively reasonable prices. It was a marginally better choice than the political statement option, but only just, and I was about to turn back into the shop and settle for an item the only disadvantage of which was that it was in silage green when I heard my name called from across the street.

It was Tiggy, who was standing with her usual group of admiring young men, eight this time, including Saul, Dean, Rick and Steve. All of them were grinning, and I returned what I hoped was a cool smile as

Tiggy trotted over to me, sailing blithely between the slow-moving traffic.

'Hi Hazel. Retail therapy?'

'Not really, no. I'm trying to buy an evening dress and I'm not having a lot of luck.'

'I know, it's crap around here, isn't it? What's the occasion?'

'A college dinner at Cambridge, this Friday.'

'Why not pick something up there then? There's Miranda, and Too Much, and Heatherbelle, or maybe Alana Swann if it's one of these high-table jobs. You can't go wrong.'

'That's a really good idea, as it goes. The last one sounds about right. What did you say they're called?'

'Alana Swann, in Trinity Lane. They're a bit old-fashioned, but if you're out to impress a load of mouldering old dons they're the best bet. Sorry, I don't mean to sound disrespectful.'

'Not at all.'

She'd looked worried, but only for a moment, and her bright smile came back before she went on.

'Or we could try Down and Out, if you don't mind?'

'The charity shop in Ellis Street? No, I don't mind, on the contrary, but do they do that sort of thing?'

'I found my gown for the summer ball there, and we might get lucky.'

She would have gone on, but the entire pack of her admirers had come over. Saul tried to squeeze her bottom and she gave him a friendly slap to get his hand away. I found myself glancing up and down the street, not really wanting to add fuel to any rumours that might be going around. Nobody I knew was visible, but I was still feeling a touch uneasy as they clustered around. Dean spoke up.

'So when do we get to party at your place, Hazel?'

Tiggy answered before I could find the right reply.

'Behave yourself, Dean. We're going shopping, so I'll see you boys later.'

'You're not coming down to the Beehive?'

'I might, later.'

She stepped away from them and they stayed put. I followed her, very much aware that they had more respect for her than they did for me. No doubt it was all down to perceived status and I was too used to the deference of students, but it still felt a little odd. After all, while I now counted Tiggy as a friend, there was still an imbalance between us, and always would be, yet the boys clearly made no such distinction.

I knew I shouldn't either, and would very much like to have broken down what remained of the barrier between us, except that I was concerned for the possible consequences. As it was I was finding it increasingly difficulty to keep my feelings for her out of my mind as she and I walked towards Ellis Street. She clearly had no such difficulties, although from the occasional comment it was plain she still saw me first and foremost as her tutor, and if Dean and his friends had told her what had happened on the heath it didn't seem to have made any difference.

We were discussing changes in urban bird population until we reached Ellis Street, where Down and Out stood among a line of shops beneath a two-storey terrace. I had occasionally shopped there, and more often given them donations, but I had no idea they might have been worth a look for an evening dress. They had three, on a rack halfway down the long, narrow shop, which the elderly lady behind the counter indicated to us before going back to her phone conversation. Two of them were plainly no use, a cream affair with sequins sewn into the bodice, that looked as if it might have been worn as part of a circus act, and a black number with a short, flounced skirt that I simply could not see myself in. A third was at least possible, a full-length gown in deep-green silk with black cotton lace across the bodice. Tiggy fastened onto the green immediately, lifting it from the rack.

'How about this?'

'It seems rather extravagant for a dinner. I'd feel overdressed.'

'I think it would look good on you, and it's about your size.'

Still doubtful, I checked the label, to discover that it was Japanese. It was also natural fibre, and only thirty pounds, but I still hesitated, imagining myself turning up as if I was going to a ball to find all the other women there in casual dress. Tiggy had turned her attention to the black dress, holding it against herself.

'What do you think of this?'

'It's not for me, too short.'

'Oh, I don't know. Maybe not for Cambridge. Are you going to try that on?'

'Um . . . yes, why not.'

They had a booth, of sorts, about two feet square and closed off with a threadbare curtain. The assistant was still talking to her friend and didn't seem to mind what we did, so I went in, handing Tiggy the dress as there wasn't even a peg to hang it on. As I began to undress I was feeling more than a little awkward. Normally going in my underwear in front of another woman would have been a matter of complete indifference, naked even, but this was Tiggy. As I stripped it was impossible not to remember how I'd imagined doing just the same so that I could be made to go down on my knees to her in front of an audience.

I might not have had an audience, but I was really

undressing, with her just a yard away, chatting happily about this and that, blissfully unaware of my feelings. The dress was my size, but would be quite tight, and was also strapless, so I knew I had an excuse to take off my bra. I knew how that would make me feel too, but the opportunity was too good to miss. Feeling somewhat guilty and somewhat foolish, I unfastened the catch, slipped the straps off, took the cups away and I was bare-breasted in front of her, my nipples achingly hard.

As I pulled back the curtain to take the dress her eyes flicked to my chest, the same stealthy glance I was used to from men, but from her merely a casual interest, a comparison but no more. That didn't stop my imagination working, making me think how it would feel to have to stand stock still, perhaps with my hands on my head, perhaps even restrained in some way, as she casually inspected my body.

'I've undone the zip for you.'

'Yes. Thank you.'

My fingers were trembling a little as I pulled the dress on over my head, and with my face lost in the folds of material I allowed myself a wry grin for my own dirty thoughts. It had been rather good, and there were a dozen ways I could enlarge on the fantasy once I was home and safely alone in bed, all of them enticing. As I adjusted the bodice I was telling myself it was foolish even to feel guilty. No harm would be done, and nobody need know. Nobody would know, for definite.

The fit was remarkably good, if not perfect, snug on my hips, but perhaps an inch too loose at the waist and rather too tight around the bust, making it easy to start the zip, yet not so easy to get it all the way up. I struggled for a second, fighting to get my fingers around to the most awkward place of all, at the very centre of my back before I surrendered to the inevitable.

'Tiggy, would you mind helping with the zip?'

'Sure.'

She tugged the curtain aside, her fingers closing on the back of my dress to pinch it together and ease the zip slowly up the last six inches as I drew in my breath.

'How is it?'

'Almost perfect, just a little tight in the bust. Let me see.'

I stepped out to admire myself in the mirror, and I had to admit it worked. A couple of tiny darts at the waist and it would follow my figure exactly, while if it was a little tight at the top that didn't do my bust any harm. The only possible drawback was that I would be overdressed, or start giving old Dr Davis-Brown ideas, but that I could cope with without difficulty. Tiggy seemed equally impressed.

'It's beautiful, you should take it.'

'Thank you, I will.'

Perhaps the glow of pleasure at her praise shouldn't have been entirely unexpected, but it was, making me feel pleasantly warm and wishing I could dare something more to fuel my fantasy. I could, just a little. The assistant was still on the phone, nobody else was in the shop anyway, and two large circular racks of coats hid us from the door. I turned my back to Tiggy.

'Could you?'

She took hold of my zip immediately, tugging it down, not just a little way either, but right to the bottom, her fingers briefly pressing against the sensitive skin at the base of my spine to send a tiny shock through me. One movement and I'd be near naked in front of her, in just my knickers while she remained fully dressed.

'Let me help.'

As she spoke she'd taken hold of the sides of my dress, and she simply tugged it down, leaving my naked breasts showing, and more as she helped me to step out of the skirts. This time the shock that ran through me was electric, enough to make me shiver. I skipped quickly back into the booth, feeling guilty and confused but now intensely aroused, far more so than such a small thing would have normally warranted, even from a man.

I was shaking badly as I closed the curtain again, and playing that brief instant over and over in my mind, when she'd caught hold of my bodice and casually tugged it down, exposing me, stripping me. Already I wanted to touch myself, and it wouldn't have taken long. It was also impossible, with the curtain hopelessly inadequate, although the thought of masturbating in front of her, even with her so close, drove my feelings higher still.

Only she'd gone, back to the rack to look at the short black dress she liked, her pale hair visible over the top of a display of dufflecoats. It was too much, I had to do it. Even as I tugged the curtain closed my hand was in the V between my legs, rubbing myself urgently through my knickers. A thrill of danger rose up inside me, as strong as my arousal, to think what a risk I was taking, and how rude I was being, masturbating in the changing booth of a charity shop because I'd been partially naked in front of another woman.

It was more than that, so much more. Tiggy was not just any woman, but the only woman for whom I'd felt any real sexual attraction, and no normal attraction. I didn't want to hold her and kiss her as equals; I wanted to go down on my knees in front of her as she sipped Champagne, stark naked, my hands lashed tight behind my back as I served her with my tongue. I wanted her to enjoy herself with some beautiful man and have me as her fluffer. I wanted her to put me across her knee and spank my bottom as a punishment, preferably in front of other people. I wanted her to make me undress in public, no, to strip me, tugging down my dress to leave me naked and vulnerable, and she had.

The moment I came I knew I'd taken a terrible risk, and I was blushing furiously and shaking with reaction for my own behaviour as I dressed, berating myself for getting so carried away and immensely grateful that I hadn't been caught. Once I'd closed my eyes with my climax rising in my head I'd been lost to everything, and if Tiggy had come back and opened the curtain . . .

It didn't bear thinking about.

She didn't, but what she did do made my feelings considerably worse. I was half dressed by the time she came back, holding not only the short black dress but two skirts, one in pleated muslin and printed with huge red poppies, the other knee-length leather, tight, and completely unsuitable for anything except showing off her figure. She tried on all three, peeling down to her underwear with casual indifference, the curtain only half closed and, when it came to the dress, taking off her bra just as I had done.

By the time we left the shop I had no choice but to admit it to myself. My desire for Tiggy went far beyond seeing her as a vehicle for my fantasies of submission to establishment and authority. I wanted her to take charge of me, yes, but I wanted her as a woman as well, in every way.

10

Just living in the same house as Tiggy became a strain over the week, but I could hardly ask her to leave because I'd fallen in love with her. I had to put up with it, wishing earnestly that the world was a simpler place and that I had as much control over my feelings as I did over my actions. She was also in every single evening, finishing her assignment, which at least saved me from reading more of her diary.

Friday night would have been disastrous, as she was going out for a meal with Gareth, and I'd had a nasty shock at lunchtime. Walking back from the refectory I caught a glimpse of two people going up the steps of the Sociology Building, and while it had only been a moment before they went inside there had been no mistaking the intimacy of their clasped hands, nor their identity – Robert and Eve.

Now I could see exactly what she'd been getting at when she kept asking me if I wanted Robert back, to check if the way was clear. Logically, I knew I had no reason to be angry, and if anything should have been grateful for the consideration she had shown me, but it was impossible not to be hurt, and suspicious. She was one of my closest friends, and I had never for a moment guessed she was keen on him, Robert and I had always had an open relationship, at least in theory, and yet looking back it was impossible not to think of all the times they'd been alone together.

I was very grateful indeed for the invitation to

Cambridge and a chance to put Tiggy, Robert, Eve and everything to do with Keynes right out of my mind. In fact, seeing them together had restored my rebellious mood, and as I had my dress and an overnight bag to transport it made sense to take the car into Cambridge. Dr Davis-Brown had reserved me a space in the fellows' car park in any event, as well as a room in college.

Principles aside, I enjoy driving, at least when out in the countryside, and with surprisingly light traffic on the A14 I had soon blown the cobwebs out of my hair and could see that Robert and Eve getting together was the best thing that could possibly have happened. Now I no longer needed to feel guilty about him, and could be with whom I pleased, when I pleased, Tiggy always excepted.

It took me a while to find the entrance to Merton fellows' car park, which was in a medieval courtyard, creating a striking contrast: the weathered gargoyles and gothic pinnacles surrounding the cluster of colourful cars, although one or two of them looked as if they weren't a great deal younger than the college. An exception was a huge silver Jaguar, brand new, just the sort of thing I'd been fighting to have prohibited for years, but with a subversive appeal. It even had a personalised number plate, a true touch of vulgar extravagance.

The lodge directed me to staircase five in St Swithun's Court, the porter even offering to carry my bag, which I declined. My rooms weren't quite as imposing as Dr Davis-Brown's set, but not by a great deal. There was a small sitting room and a bedroom with a tiny bathroom tucked into one corner, all very new and a greater deal better than anything we were able to offer even our graduate students at Keynes. I was on the third floor too, with a view of jumbled rooftops of yellow stone and lead, adding to the air of scholarship and antiquity. I tried to tell myself it was just an example of academic inequality, but I knew all the stock arguments and found it hard to when Merton had been there for nearly five hundred years.

I had plenty of time, and took a leisurely shower before lying down to read for a while in a pleasant, half-waking state which I only came out of when the university bells began to chime seven o'clock. Already I felt a world away from Keynes, and that became stronger as I slipped into my gown. It had been a good choice, very much in keeping with the old college and made me feel elegant and curiously timeless as I took in my reflection in the mirror.

Walking through the college my sense of detachment grew stronger still. I might have taken the same walk, in the same dress, at any time in the last fifty years, maybe nearer a hundred, and nothing would have changed, while the college had been much the same for another hundred before that, perhaps longer. I'd imagined the hall as a sort of medieval banqueting chamber, hung with flags and set around with suits of mail and trophies of arms. The reality wasn't far off, dark wood, stone and stained glass, with portraits of past Masters of the college looking down on rows of tables already set out, and with rowing trophies in place of those of war.

It would have been hard to imagine anything more patriarchal, more establishment, more reactionary, and yet I found it impossible to resent. Those students who were at the main tables were evenly balanced between male and female, with the accents of Liverpool and Newcastle commoner than the plummy voices I had expected. Even among those at the top table three were women, and they carried all the scholarship of their male counterparts, including Dr Davis-Brown, who greeted me with a cheerful wave and beckoned me to a chair at the end of the high table.

'Ah, Dr Jones, and very charming you look, if I may say so. Do sit down, and perhaps a few introductions would be in order.'

He began to indicate the other people at the table, beginning with the Master and ending with a man my own age, or perhaps a little more, who was seated to my left.

'...and my other guest, Miles Shelldrake, with whom you have a good deal in common. Miles was a student of mine in the late eighties, but sadly could not be persuaded to progress.'

Miles Shelldrake rather took the eye, and I found myself flushing a trifle as he offered his hand. Not only was he in immaculate black tie that put most of the dons to shame, but he clearly had most of the characteristics of my archetypal male, including height, a slender yet powerful build, and most importantly that same air of self-confidence I knew so well in Tiggy. He also had a mop of loose black hair, dark, intense eyes and a smile that suggested in his mind he already had me stripped and kneeling at his feet. I was vaguely aware that Dr Davis-Brown was still speaking.

'Miles is now with MacDouglas Alpha.'

I recognised the name immediately, the oil exploration company Dr Davis-Brown had mentioned in his letter. Had he told me Miles was the Christian Devil it couldn't have been a sharper shock to the fantasy I'd already been evolving in my head, because Miles didn't just look like the man I should have at once hated and wanted to grovel to, to all intents and purposes he was that man. If I'd been sat down next to the Master of the Breckland and Fen I couldn't have felt any more uncomfortable and it was only a sense of politeness towards Dr Davis-Brown that prevented me from making some appropriate remark. At the least I had to say something.

'I'm Senior Lecturer in Environmental Biology at Keynes.'

His grin had become a positive smirk as he replied.

'So I believe. You gave evidence to the Twelve Mile enquiry, didn't you?'

'Yes, I did.'

He gave a chuckle.

'After I'd read the report I was astonished to discover that the redoubtable Dr H Jones was a woman, but it's hardly polite to rake over old enmities when we're both guests of Edward's. Have you dined in Merton before?'

I'd opened my mouth to point out that my being a woman was irrelevant to my ability to act as an expert witness, but shut it again, neatly cut off.

'No, I haven't.'

It was only then that it occurred to me that there was no sign of a menu, or anything to suggest that we would have a vegetarian choice, something at Keynes I took for granted. I could only hope that Dr Davis-Brown had remembered, and that I'd be spared the embarrassment of having to send anything back. To judge by what Miles Shelldrake was saying that might have to be the entire meal.

'. . . very possibly the best kitchens in Cambridge, to say nothing of an excellent cellar. Our current chef even did a stint in *Aux Armes de France*, which provides an occasional hint of Alsatian flair, and I believe he still imports his *foie gras* from the same supplier. Apparently we're having it tonight.'

That was really too much.

'I couldn't possibly eat *foie gras*, even if I wasn't strictly vegetarian.'

'You're vegetarian? Good Heavens, you don't know what you're missing. At least have a taste; I'm sure you'll be converted.'

'Absolutely not!'

'Suit yourself, just as long as you don't mind the rest of us tucking in.'

'I do, as a matter of fact, but as a guest I'm prepared to accept it.'

'Why? Surely if you want me to accept your moral position, then you should accept mine?'

'That hardly applies in this case. Imagine if somebody you know made a habit of shooting a random stranger every day. Wouldn't you object?'

'Yes, certainly.'

'Then you might begin to understand how I feel about eating the flesh of animals, especially animal raised and killed specifically for human consumption, to say nothing of the cruelty involved in this case.'

I thought he'd reply, and have the whole argument neatly laid out, ready for whatever response he chose. Instead he merely gave his head the very slightest of shakes, as if to dismiss my viewpoint as so far detached from reason that it didn't deserve a response. Again I was forced to bite my tongue, not wishing to get into a full-blown argument. Fortunately Dr Davis-Brown came to my rescue with surprising tact.

'I did remember your, um … predilection, Hazel – if I may call you Hazel – and I've asked chef to make appropriate arrangements.'

'Thank you, Dr Davis-Brown … Edward, that's very considerate of you.'

'Think nothing of it. So many of the students seem to expect it these days that it's really no trouble at all.

I trust you'll join us in asparagus and stilton soup? It's cooked with butter, naturally, but purely organic, from a pedigree Jersey herd on our land in Somerset.'

I didn't have the heart to refuse, telling myself it wasn't actually meat, and a waiter had arrived in any case, to slide a bowl of thick green soup neatly into place in front of me. It smelt delicious, and tasted better still, which only added to my guilt. The bread served with it was also excellent, and the delicate, perfumed white wine like nothing I had ever drunk before.

Miles Shelldrake had turned his attention to his other neighbour, doubtless deciding that I wasn't worth talking too, while I had determinedly pushed all thought of his erotic possibilities from my mind. He was just the sort of arrogant, self-satisfied bastard I'd always hated, and as with the huntsmen and farm boys of the Breckland and Fen, the reality was very different to the fantasy.

My opinion was strengthened by the next course, a walnut salad for me, and individual quail in a rich yellow jelly for everybody else, which he ate with all the repulsive gusto of a stone-age man devouring raw meat. Unfortunately it smelt absolutely delicious, more tempting even than the bacon sandwiches which had hitherto provided me with the strongest temptation.

I was at least distracted by the excellent wine, another white but rich and heavy, and by Edward Davis-Brown's reminiscences of work with the British Antarctic Survey in the sixties, something that had always fascinated me and one of the reasons I'd been drawn into environmental science. He'd also been to Greenland, as I had, at last allowing me to make a worthwhile contribution to the conversation.

'. . . two years ago, although where I was working would have been under ice when you visited.'

'No doubt, although at the time the glacier had been in retreat for the best part of a hundred years. After all, it was a text book example of succession in the fifties.'

'That's true, but I'm sure even Miles would admit that the rate has been increasing.'

Miles looked up from the last of his quail in aspic.

'I admit it freely, and also that it is a serious problem. What we disagree on is the solution. My company wishes to move slowly towards an economically viable situation in which humanity can maintain progress. You green types want to return us to the stone age.'

'That's not true at all!'

'Isn't it? Let's take an example. Am I right in think that you'd rather people had horses than private cars?'

'No.'

'No? I understood that the abolition of the private car was one of your principle shibboleths?'

'OK. First of all, it's a mistake to lump everybody with environmental concerns in under the same umbrella. I for one take a balanced viewpoint.'

'Balanced, but weighted according to your personal preconceptions.'

'Which are carefully considered and relate to the long-term benefit of both humanity and the planet, rather than short-term gain. As for cars and horses, even well after the second world war infection due to fly bites caused more deaths in London alone every single year than are currently caused by road traffic accidents. So no, I'm not in favour of us all using horses. I'd prefer to see a proper level of investment in electrically powered cars, also smaller, less inefficient engines and lower speeds. We don't need to charge around the country in gigantic vehicles, like yours, I suspect?'

I'd guessed the Jaguar in the car park was probably his, but if so my remark failed to hit home. He dabbed his mouth with his napkin and took a sip of wine before replying.

'Good answer. You think, I'll grant you that. Have you ever considered moving into the private sector?'

'No.'

'Why not?'

'Because I would have to say what I was paid to say rather than what I think.'

'How much would it take to change you mind?'

'Not everybody is obsessed with money, Mr Shelldrake.'

'Everybody has their price, myself included. What are you earning now?'

'I'd rather not say.'

'What's the top of your scale nowadays then, thirty-six? Thirty-eight?'

'Thereabouts.'

'And you get by on that?'

'Well enough, yes.'

'Let's say your finances balance. How would an extra twenty thousand feel? Think of what you could do.'

'Is that an offer, Mr Shelldrake?'

'No, not as such, but we are looking for an environmental spokesman and we need somebody who won't wilt the first time they have to talk to the press, the boss, or some psycho from an action group. You'd be ideal.'

'Possibly I'm the psycho from the action group, though?'

'Oh no, you're far too sensible. You think about your actions. Did you know that some lunatic released several hundred mink from a farm in Buckinghamshire the other day? That's the sort of stupid behaviour I mean. I don't see you doing that.'

'I wouldn't, it's true, because the damage far outweighs the benefits, but I believe the same is true of much of what your company does.'

'Now there we must agree to differ. Are you sure you won't try the *foi gras*? Believe me, with a glass of the eighty-eight Rieussec the combination of flavours will be superb.'

'No. Thank you. But I will try the wine.'

The *foi gras* was being served, only it wasn't a paté, but individual slices of whole liver, and recognisable as such. I looked quickly away as Miles was served and raised my hand to make doubly sure I wasn't given any. A different waiter brought me a beautifully presented dish, a single red pepper stuffed and roasted with pine kernels and ceps, and yet another poured me a glass of deep golden wine. Both were delicious, but as I put my glass down I realised that the entire table had gone quiet, the buzz of conversation dying to nothing in the space of a few seconds.

I looked up, wondering if I'd committed some awful social gaffe, to find that every single person at the high table was lost in what can only be described as rapture as they carefully took in tiny pieces of *foi gras* and sips of the sweet, heavy wine. I had never seen anything so decadent, nor so gluttonous, and Dr Davis-Brown was no exception, while Miles looked as if he was about to have an orgasm. Barely a word was spoken until they'd finished, when Miles gave a sigh of immense satisfaction and took up more or less where he'd left off.

'That is the essence of gustatory pleasure, although perhaps a few fresh grapes might have added a last perfect touch. The art is in the combination, you see.

As I hope you'll agree, the wine is superb, and so is the *foi gras*, yet the pleasure of the whole far, far exceeds the sum of the parts.

'What about the poor goose, and don't you even feel guilty, stuffing yourself with delicious things when more than half the world population is living in poverty?'

'No, and this is a *foi gras de canard*, duck.'

I declined to answer, sure that nothing I could say to a man of his supreme arrogance would make the slightest difference, while I had no wish to be seen as somebody who did nothing but argue. Besides, I'd already eaten three courses myself, and nothing remotely resembling a main course had arrived. Nor did it next, only tiny bowls of jasmine-scented sorbet, the purpose of which Miles hastened to explain.

'After such rich flavours you need to refresh your palate, otherwise you won't be able to appreciate the main course.'

'I see, and what is the main course?'

'In your case I have no idea, probably tofu on wild rice. We are having suckling pig.'

He smacked his lips as he pronounced the words, and at the same moment I caught the scent of roast pork, every bit as enticing as bacon, but I couldn't bear to look. I really was back in the middle ages, with habits to suit, the meal at once so extravagant and so grotesque that I couldn't help but wonder if they'd selected the menu as some sort of test, or simply to horrify me. Unfortunately it seemed more likely that they ate the same way every night.

Nor did they seem to have the slightest awareness that their behaviour might be questionable, smacking their lips and murmuring compliments on the food as they devoured it with no more sense of higher feeling than a group of hyena around a wildebeest carcass. I ate my own nut roast in stolid silence, replying only to direct questions, and with an ever-increasing sense of indignation. After all, the scent was just as alluring to me as to them, yet I was capable of holding back.

Wine was being poured with a liberal hand, some rich, delicious and no doubt hideously expensive red. I didn't hold back, sure that getting partially drunk was the best way to get through the awful meal. It only made things worse, heightening my emotions and yet weakening my resistance to the allure of Miles Shelldrake, whose remarks had grown increasingly familiar as we ate, and were peppered with what he presumably thought were compliments.

'I must say, Hazel, you have a remarkably good figure for a vegetarian. I'd always assumed an inadequate diet would leave you all skin and bones.'

'There's nothing inadequate about a vegetarian diet, it simply needs to be properly balanced.'

'Maybe, although to me it just seems such a pointless exercise.'

'It must be nice not to suffer from a social conscience.'

'That's not entirely fair. If I lacked all conscience I would . . . no, I had better not say.'

'Why not?'

'I have no wish to offend you, although by any objective criteria it would have been complimentary.'

I could guess what he meant, that he would have made some remark about his reaction to me, perhaps even implying that if he really had no conscience he would have simply taken me then and there. I could also see the trap, my refutation, followed by his denial of intent, leaving me the one who had brought up the possibility of sex between us.

'I'm not entirely naïve, Mr Shelldrake.'

He laughed.

'So I see, and do call me Miles.'

Clearly he was enjoying the game, and would have that same smug little smile on his face if I grew angry, if I was cold to him, and all the more if I ended up in bed with him. It was hard to see a satisfactory way out, short of taking somebody he would consider far less attractive than himself to bed in his place, and that rather defeated the object. It was still tempting, but unfortunately the next most appealing man on our table was over fifty, overweight and had a face like a halibut into the bargain.

It was better by far to simply behave in as neutral a fashion as possible, refusing to rise to the bait in any way whatsoever, and I determined to do so. What I thought privately, or did privately, was another matter, as he would never know. That was for me alone, and all the more so because as he continued to talk and to give his opinion on different topics with ever greater self-assurance as he drank my true reaction would have amused him immensely. By the time a pudding of apricot tart smothered in cream had been served I didn't know if I wanted to slap his face for him, or go down under the table and suck his cock.

They'd creamed my tart as well, apparently assuming I simply didn't eat meat, but I was feeling too drunk and too fragile to protest. It was delicious too, as was the wine, another sweet one, and the fifth I'd had, making me very glad indeed it was the end. Only it wasn't. Cheese followed, a huge board loaded with stilton, cheddar, brie, camembert and several I didn't recognise. I declined, only to discover that Edward Davis-Brown had filled my glass with port as I spoke to the waiter.

Miles Shelldrake continued to flirt, his determination growing stronger as I continued to give calm, matter of fact answers. To make it worse, our near neighbours had become engrossed in a conversation on college politics, leaving him and me on our own, and I was very glad indeed when the meal finally came to an end. Edward Davis-Brown spoke as he pushed back his chair.

'Splendid. We adjourn to the senior common room for coffee, if you'd care to join us, Hazel?'

Coffee was exactly what I needed, also a chance to speak to somebody other than Miles Shelldrake. Not that it would be easy, with the dons deep in debate on college matters, while some ancient and pointless piece of protocol demanded that we leave in procession, with the Master at the head. As guests, Miles and I came last, with him now expounding his theory of male dominance in modern society.

'... superficially, yes, male roles may seem to have changed, but in practice it's simply that the beta-males are able to justify their subservient condition by taking up feminist concepts, thus saving face. The alpha males continue as they always have, firmly in charge.'

'That theory is not only out of date but was extremely weak in the first place, as I'm sure you know.'

'Strictly pop science, I'll grant you, but it illustrates the situation well enough. After all, you only have to look at the political scene to see that nothing has changed, Maggie always excepted. I imagine that was all rather awkward for your lot, having the first ever female Prime Minister on the opposite side?'

'Not entirely, no, but she's not the only example. Things are changing, with more women MPs than ever before.'

'Only because they're parachuted in by a politically correct leadership, along with all women shortlists, and that's the route to disaster. Besides, look what happened with that woman in Cardiff last time ... or was it Swansea?'

'Blaenau Gwent, I suppose you mean?'

'I knew it was somewhere like that.'

I had to try something to prick his pomposity.

'So how do you see yourself fitting in, rather like Michael Caine in *Alfie*, I suppose?'

'Not at all.'

'No?'

'Absolutely. He's ghastly.'

'I'd have thought he'd be something of a role model for you?'

'Please, insult me as you will, but credit me with some intelligence. Not that we should take these morality tales seriously, in any case. They merely reflect modern preoccupations, and in the most simplistic way, and no, I don't see myself in the character at all. To make the story work it is essential that the man is a fool, practically half-witted in fact, especially in the remake with Jude Law. He doesn't know his own mind, but simply uses what little sense he has to justify following his primitive instincts, and then gets upset about it when things don't go his way.'

'I suppose you would have done better?'

'Oh absolutely. There'd be none of this nonsense about abortion for a start. If they're fool enough to get pregnant, let them have babies, that's what I say.'

He'd timed it perfectly, making the most outrageous remark just as we reached the senior common room, so that as Edward Davis Brown ushered us in I was unable to give him the reply he deserved. The moment was lost as the three of us went to the table on which coffee and decanters of spirits had been laid out, and we separated as I accepted a cup from yet another waiter and Shelldrake poured himself a generous measure of what looked like brandy. Edward was also having coffee, and spoke to me as we stepped away from the table.

'If you drop in on me before you leave tomorrow I have all three of the theses you're examining.'

'Thank you. You seem to have three very able students there.'

'Yes, I think so. Ray I'm sure will continue in the field, and almost certainly Phil Paddon.'

'He seems very keen.'

'Absolutely. I've never known a man like him for work. Never stops. Will you have a mint?'

I took one and we continued to talk, the amount of drink I'd had making everything seem a little unreal, as if the dons had no more substance than the portraits of their predecessors on the walls. It was a dangerous condition to be in, with Miles Shelldrake around, and I finished my coffee and made my excuses as soon as I decently could, eager to reach the sanctuary of my room. I'd got as far as saying goodnight to Edward when Miles appeared at my shoulder.

'Leaving already, Hazel?'

'Yes. I have to drive back in the morning.'

He took the rest of his brandy at a single swallow before replying.

'I believe we're on the same stair, so I'll also say goodnight, and take the liberty of escorting you back.'

He was like Mr Wolf toying with Little Red Riding Hood, his wicked grin a dead giveaway of his intentions, although in this case I suspected he was thinking of me eating him rather than the other way around. I wasn't falling for it, despite what my body was telling me, and carefully detached myself as he tried to take my arm. He took no notice, still talking as we followed the turn of the cloistered walk around the main court, our footsteps loud on the worn stone slabs.

A narrow passage led to St Swithun's Court, unlit and gloomy, just the sort of place to take hold of me and kiss me, something I knew I'd find hard to resist. He didn't, nor on the stair where a narrow stone landing separated our rooms, merely smiling as he paused outside his door.

'I think the choice is yours, Dr Jones. We're both mature adults, and I'm sure we both want the same thing, so if you are willing to set aside the antipathy you so evidently feel for me and join me, man and woman, that would be a pleasure. Why go to a lonely bed if you don't have to?'

I drew my breath in.

'Mr Shelldrake. It may surprise you to discover that I do not find you as fascinating as you seem to think. In fact I think it is fair to say that of all the men I have ever met you are the most arrogant, obnoxious, and downright rude, while I have no desire whatsoever to go to bed with you. Good night.'

If I'd made the slightest dent in his armour it didn't show. His response was the slightest of shrugs and a condescending little smile before he turned to his door and I to mine. In the safety of my room I let my relief sweep over me. I'd resisted my own darkest desires, and when drunk at that. I locked the door and began to undress, my pride intact but my arousal bubbling inside me.

There was really no choice but to masturbate, and I knew if I tried to go to sleep instead I would simply end up tossing and turning until my need overcame me. It was better to enjoy myself and be content that he would never know what he had driven me to. Naked, I crossed to my bed and lay down, only to think better of it. As with Tiggy, Miles provoked a desire in me to kneel at his feet, and that would undoubtedly be the best way to come.

My armchair was perfect, and all the better because there would presumably be one just like it in the room next door. Possibly he was even seated in it, reading a novel before bed. As I got down on the floor I was imagining how it would feel to go in, to find him seated in his chair, still fully dressed in his dinner jacket. He'd look up, his face full of haughty amusement, maybe even a touch of contempt.

He'd tell me I'd had my chance and if I wanted him now I'd have to strip and crawl to him on all fours. I was already naked, and I began to act out the scene, picturing him watching me from the armchair as I grovelled to him. He'd pull out his cock, holding it up for my mouth, cool and arrogant as he told me what I had to do, lick and suck until he was ready before he tied me up and made full use of my helpless body.

I reached the chair and knelt in front of it, my eyes closed as my hands slipped down between my thighs. It was going to be good, the very essence of my fantasies, and over a real man, an absolute bastard, just the sort who really would have done all the things I like best, and who was only next door, and had invited me in. I could go, so easily, and it would become real . . .

No. I wouldn't do it. I wouldn't give him the satisfaction.

Yet he had appealed to me as a woman, daring me to set aside our differences and react by instinct. It was unspeakably arrogant of him to assume he had aroused me, but it was true. I did want to be with him, and in a way that would probably have surprised him, even shocked him. That was what decided me, because I knew exactly what he'd be thinking, that I was cold and prissy, too wrapped up in my own world to express myself as a woman, maybe just about capable of, say, going on top, and then only in a nice, safe situation. He had a shock coming.

I got up, made a few adjustments to my face and hair and slipped on my robe. There was some self doubt, some conscience, and the knowledge that had I drunk less wine I'd never have dared, but none of that stopped me. I slipped out onto the landing and across, knocking gently and pushing the door wide without waiting for a reply. Miles was still fully dressed, just as I'd imagined him, only not seated but standing by the fireplace to admire the rowing trophy fixed above it. He smiled as he saw it was me.

'I had hoped you might change your mind.'

'Don't be too flattered, Miles. It's just that I have this thing about male chauvinist pigs. You happen to be a prize specimen, and that's how I want you to behave.'

This was no Robert. His smile grew broader, more wicked.

'Oh, I think I can cope with that.'

I wanted him to tell me what to do, or order me naked to my knees and onto his cock. He didn't, but simply put one elbow up on the mantelpiece, watching with his mouth set into a faint smirk as I locked the door. As I turned again I let my robe slip from my shoulders and I was naked. His eyes flicked down my body, in amusement, pleasure, and surprise as I got down on all fours, but only for a moment before he spoke.

'Very appropriate. Come on then, good girl, good doggie, crawl to Daddy.'

He was treating me as a dog, a thought that sent a

jolt through me, so sharp it made me falter, intense outrage warring with a yet stronger desire. It was beyond anything I had imagined, supremely dominant, and far, far too good to resist. I was going to do it. I was doing it, crawling naked across the floor to a man's feet, and as I reached him I nuzzled my cheek against his leg, and higher, to feel the already stiffening bulk of his cock through his dress trousers. He looked down, his eyes glittering with pleasure as his hands went to his flies.

'Does Fifi want a bone?'

I nodded and once again rubbed my face into his crotch. He gave a soft chuckle and his zip was down. My mouth came wide, my legs and hands up and I was begging for it, lost in an ecstasy of submission beyond anything before as I pretended to be his dog, his bitch. Out came his cock, into my mouth and I was sucking, my eyes closed in bliss as he quickly began to grow hard. His fingers touched my hair, ruffling it.

'Good girl, Fifi. That's right, just like that.'

Again he ruffled my hair, praising me just as if I really was his dog, before taking a firm grip and pulling himself deeper into my mouth. I did my best to respond, sucking eagerly and toying with the heavy sac of his balls, all the while with my arousal soaring higher and higher still. He had it so right, immediately taking me beyond the limits of my own imagination by making me his bitch. I'd done it too, accepting the role and crawling naked to his feet, begging to be allowed to suck on his beautiful cock, now stiff in my mouth. I already needed to come, badly, but as I gave in and my hands went lower he gave a little tut and spoke.

'Uh, uh, oh no you don't, Fifi. We'll have none of that dirty behaviour.'

I nodded and took my hands away, placing them on the floor as he moved my head back a little to watch me suck and pull at his cock as I did it. At his command my frustration had immediately begun to rise, making my desire stronger still because I was under orders. All it needed for perfection was one final detail, and as he finally eased me back I found my voice.

'If you don't want me to touch myself, I think you'd better tie my hands.'

His smirk grew positively diabolic.

'An excellent idea, and who'd have thought it, eh? The oh-so-proper Dr Hazel Jones a bondage baby.'

'Not Dr Jones, not Hazel. Fifi.'

'Fifi it is, but before I tie you I'm going to fuck you, doggy style. Get on the bed, come on, up girl, good girl!'

As he'd spoken I'd jumped up on the bed, now completely lost to his will as I got onto all fours, my bottom presented to him just as he'd ordered. He climbed on behind me, his hands found my flesh, taking a firm hold on my hips. I felt his cock touch and he was in me, pushed deep to fill me right to the top of my head. I was already clutching the bedclothes as he began to thrust into me, lost to everything decent and proper and dignified as I played his bitch, naked on all fours as he drove into me from behind, fucked doggy style.

I couldn't help it. One hand had gone back between my legs before he'd even got his rhythm properly and I was masturbating, desperate to bring myself to ecstasy as I was treated in such a wonderfully rude way. He let me, maybe himself too excited to care, my fingers sending shocks of ecstasy through me in perfect time to the thrusts of his cock as my pleasure rode higher. He stopped, suddenly.

'Uh, uh, bad Fifi, what did I say? What did I say about playing with yourself, you dirty girl?'

'Not to.'

My voice was a sigh as I answered. It felt so good to be told off, as a bad dog, and I knew the punishment too, my favourite. As his cock eased free of my body he spoke again.

'We'll soon put a stop to that. Where's your lead?'

I looked back as he climbed off the bed, watching wide eyed as he pulled the cord from my robe. Just knowing what he was about to do with it made me melt completely, and as he came back my hands were already crossed in the small of my back, with my face pushed down into the bed. He chuckled as he climbed up once more, his cock brushing my thighs as he took hold of my wrists.

'Obedient little bitch at heart, aren't you, Fifi? Now let's get you bound.'

He moved, and to my surprise and delight he had slid his cock back into my body even as he began to work on my wrists. I was being tied and fucked at the same time, another exquisite detail to build on, so good I was wriggling myself onto him as I was rendered helpless. He laughed and slapped my bottom for my eagerness.

'Bad girl, Fifi. Dirty girl, Fifi. Wait your turn.'

With my wrists lashed firmly together he took hold once more and began to fuck me properly, deep and hard. He was going to come, his breathing already harsh, his pushes harder and growing harder still, to set me gasping and biting the bedcovers to stop myself crying out loud. Every thrust of his hips was smacking onto my bottom and driving his dick to the hilt, sending shocks of pleasure through me, close to orgasm as he began to talk again.

'Oh, yes, this is good, Hazel Jones ... Fifi, my darling little bitch!'

He broke off with a grunt, jammed himself to the very hilt and I knew he'd come in me, the final delicious indignity before I was allowed to do it in front of him, masturbating on my back with my legs open to show off, or still on my knees, bottom up as I showed him exactly what he'd done to me.

It was neither. With his hard cock still pushed deep inside me he had curled a hand around under my tummy and was masturbating me, with my hands still tied. I heard my own gasp of ecstasy, immediate, and again, my orgasm already rising in my head as I played through what he done to me: made me his dog, his bitch; made me crawl to him in the nude; made me suck his penis until he was hard; made me kneel on his bed and fucked me from behind, and best ... best of all, he'd tied my hands behind my back to stop me being dirty with myself and called me his darling little bitch as he fucked me.

I yelled. How I yelled, unable to hold myself back as my orgasm tore through me, so long and so good that by the time I'd finally finished all I could do was collapse beneath him, and as he came down on top of me his mouth found mine in a lingering, open kiss.

11

When I woke in Miles Shelldrake's bed he was still asleep. Even before I'd fully recovered consciousness my thoughts and feelings were a jumble, and it was more than I could bear to have to talk to him. He had brought me to a level of ecstasy I'd only ever dreamed about, and yet the way he'd done it was impossibly inappropriate. All I wanted to do was to get away, to be alone with my own thoughts in an effort to reconcile fantasy and reality.

Before I left Merton I collected the three PhD theses, now bound and ready for my perusal before the viva, but I didn't linger. Politely declining Edward Davis-Brown's offer of breakfast in the hall I made my way to the car park. The sight of Miles's great sleek Jaguar brought my feelings back to the boil, and as I drove slowly east through the crowded Cambridge streets I didn't know if I wanted to cry, to masturbate, or both. Only when I'd picked up speed on the main road did my head finally begin to clear enough to allow myself a wry grin for my own behaviour.

It had been good, without question; the best. Unlike Robert or Dean and his friends, Miles had known what to do. I'd barely had to provide a hint, much less orchestrate everything, and he had taken over, adding his own spectacularly wicked details. Just to think of what I'd let him do – no, what I'd revelled in him doing – was enough to have me shaking my head. It was outrageous. So outrageous in fact that had anybody told Sarah, or Eve, or any of my other friends at Keynes, they'd simply have refused to believe it.

Even back at Keynes it was a great deal easier to cope with my feelings than I'd expected. Rather than worry about how inappropriate my behaviour had been and wherever I had betrayed my own values, I found myself enjoying having such a wonderful secret, no doubt much as Tiggy did for all the things she'd recorded in her diary. Not that I intended to write down what had happened, not with every detail burned into my memory.

I also had plenty to do, not least read and assess the three PhD theses. Laura Simmons's was the slimmest of the three, so I started with that, taking in a chunk each day until my concentration had begun to slip. With Tiggy still putting the finishing touches to her assignment the first few evenings of the week were quiet and studious, with both of us working and only coming together for a late-night cup of chocolate. It wasn't until the Thursday that I found myself on my own. With Tiggy and Gareth out together I was left to Laura's concise, dry prose and cod fry statistics.

By shortly before ten o'clock I'd reached the end of her data and my head was swimming with cod fry, enough to restock the entire Atlantic Ocean. I badly needed a glass of wine and I'd earned it too. To think was to act, and five minutes later I was installed in the living room with my feet up and sipping chilled white wine, which went right to the spot, and to my head.

One glass and I was thinking pleasant, gentle thoughts with a mildly erotic tone. Two glasses and I was remembering the Friday night and how I'd asked Miles to make a pig of himself with me, and he had. Three glasses and my thoughts had turned to Tiggy and how nice it would be to have her treat me the same. Four glasses and my fantasy had grown to being shared between them, fulfilling the joint roles of pet dog and sex slave. Five glasses and I was ready to go upstairs to be thoroughly naughty with myself. Six and I was on my way, the bottle now empty.

Not to have peeped into Tiggy's room would have been impossible. Not seeing her diary would have been equally impossible, as it was right at the centre of her desk. Not to read a little would have been more impossible still.

I wanted a good bit, something juicy to add to the fantasy I had already devised. Flicking through, I let my eyes feast on the wonderful details of her sex life, no longer envious to me, but still exciting. Only not exciting enough. Every single day she seemed to have done something, if only show her breasts to Gareth as he masturbated, or provide a helping hand to Saul in the back row of the cinema. Not even the times she persuaded them to tie her up or smack her bottom were right. I wanted to read about her being in charge, perhaps taking her revenge on Janice, so that I could imagine it was me.

Page after page I read, with increasing frustration and also increasing astonishment at the sheer scope of her desire. That the boys always responded was no surprise, but it didn't even seem to matter to her what time of the month it was. Perhaps stranger still were her constant references to the mysterious X, who she clearly longed for but seemed unable to approach. How could that be, when she was quite capable of making thoroughly indecent proposals to everyone from the over-sexed Saul to the quiet, studious Janice?

When I got halfway through April I found out.

Treated four of the boys to bjs for helping me move. So turned on I ended up taking them one at each end. With X most of the day, and I am now living with her.

I read it again, and a third time, but the words weren't going to change. X could only be one person, and that was me.

It was a shock, to put it mildly, but it made absolutely no difference at all, save that it was a great pity. Whatever Tiggy's feelings towards me, just as whatever my feelings towards her, she was still my student. To act on what I knew would be unthinkable, and all the more so because I'd read it in her diary. I would have to carry on as before.

That was easier said than done, now with the sure knowledge that she reciprocated my feelings and that if I did make an advance it would be accepted. Before, my assumption of rejection had made it relatively easy, but that was no longer the case, and every moment I was with her the words I knew I couldn't say were on the tip of my tongue.

The weekend might have been unbearable but for Sarah, who came round first thing on the Saturday morning with a serious expression on her face. She also had a leaflet in her hand, and had thrust it into mine almost before she was through the front door, already talking.

'It's not going to happen, not if I can help it!'

I looked at the leaflet, somewhat bemused as it was for a gay bar, something she would normally have been in favour of.

'What's not going to happen?'

'The council closing down The Cottage. It's outrageous, blatant homophobia!'

'I don't know anything about this.'

'What the bastards did was send in some snoop who managed to get a drink at one minute past two o'clock, so now they been refused a new licence. It's a set-up, pure and simple! They don't give a fuck about licensing; they just want to get at gay men without showing their true colours.'

'I suppose that's possible, but why would they bother?'

'Because of some moralising old fart of a councillor with a bad dose of Christian morals, I suspect. That doesn't matter. What does is that we have to protest it all the way, or it'll just be the tip of the iceberg. I'm organising leafleting shifts and I've got you down for this afternoon.'

'This afternoon? Sarah ...'

'Come on, Hazel, this is important. What else would you be doing?'

I didn't entirely appreciate the tone of her voice, and was going to say so, only to think better of it. My morning was busy in the department, but in the afternoon I had nothing on, and might well have ended up alone in the house with Tiggy, or riding with Dean, Saul and the others, who seemed keen to get us both out at once. It was also a cause for which I now felt a more personal sympathy.

'Nothing. You're right, it is important. I'll be there at one. Coffee?'

'No thank you, I need to finish organising my rota. Bye.'

She left, leaving me holding the leaflet for The Cottage, which showed a muscular young man in over tight lycra shorts standing outside a small white building in a park. Gay he might have been, but it was impossible not to enjoy the sculpted muscles of his body, and I began to wonder if the afternoon might prove entertaining as well as worthy.

It was, even if the men weren't quite as muscular or as scantily dressed as the one on their leaflet. They appreciated what we were doing, and immediately provided me with a chair and an offer of unlimited coffee and beer. I accepted both, sitting down to sip coffee and handing out leaflets to the few passers-by who ventured down the tiny side street in which The Cottage was located.

Occasionally the staff would come out to talk to me, or a customer share a few words before going in, but even they were few and far between. By tea-time I was beginning to wonder when I'd be relieved when a male couple approached, one a tall, powerfully built black guy, the other not quite so tall but very muscular, and familiar, although it took me a moment to recall his name.

'Hello. Josh, isn't it?'

He looked mildly surprised and I quickly introduced myself.

'I'm Hazel Jones, here to hand out leaflets protesting against the threatened closure of The Cottage. You play rugby, don't you?'

'Yes, that's right.'

'I thought I recognised you. My window overlooks the sports field.'

'Oh right! Hey, keep up the good work.'

He gave me a friendly thumbs up and went inside, leaving me somewhat puzzled. Quite clearly he was gay, unashamedly so, which was peculiar as he'd been a boyfriend of Tiggy's in the first year. Possibly he was still finding his way and had only just come to terms with his sexuality. Possibly he was bisexual and just as happy with a woman as with a man. If so, I had to admire his openness, and began to wonder if I should conceal my new-found desire for women – or at least, a woman – or make a point of being out and proud.

I had always admired those with the courage to openly declare their sexuality, and the more prejudice there was in society as a whole against their choice the more I admired them. When my own sexuality came into question it was not so black and white, especially after the disaster with Robert. Lesbianism was fine; safe, tolerated by obligation. Bisexuality was less acceptable.

Sarah, for instance, would support me but assume I was going through a transitional phase towards full lesbianism. Maybe I was. No, not after Miles Shelldrake. Perhaps it would be seen as a problem, the way Robert had seen my desire to be tied, which would be a nuisance. Supporting others was one thing. Expressing myself was quite another.

Saturday night was spent at The Cottage, along with Sarah and several others, including Robert, whose very obvious discomfort at being in a gay bar I couldn't help but find amusing. By the time I left I was sufficiently drunk to be tempted by Tiggy's diary and sufficiently tired to collapse into bed without giving in. It was just as well, because no sooner had I put *The Poor Mouth* down on my bedside table and turned out the light than I caught the dull roar of motorbike engines, growing louder and cutting off at the end of the close. Some minutes later the door catch clicked and I heard Tiggy's voice, asking softly if I was still up. I didn't reply, choosing sleep as the wise option.

She was up before me, and I woke to the smell of

toast and coffee. As we sat over breakfast I was more torn than ever between wanting to say something and my determination not to risk things getting out of hand. Gareth called for her while I was still washing up, and I was left to my own devices. I had already decided to go out, perhaps up to the heathland near Massingham, which was an excellent place to be alone with my thoughts. There I could make a clear decision based on what was best for me and for her, without allowing my emotions to get in the way.

The phone went as I was putting together a picnic lunch. I very nearly didn't answer it, imagining that it would be Sarah to ask if I could stand in for somebody at The Cottage, or maybe Robert to say things hadn't worked out with Eve and that he wanted us to try again. Only after maybe a dozen rings did my conscience get the better of me, and as I put the receiver to my ear I caught a familiar arrogant drawl – Miles Shelldrake.

'Hazel? Are you around?'

I was taken aback, not sure what to say to a man whose last words to me had been 'darling little bitch', or what he would want.

'Um . . . I was going out, but I've got a minute, yes.'

'Anything important?'

'Well . . .'

'Anything more important than letting me take you to the Fattened Goose? No, I didn't think so. I'll be there in five minutes.'

'What? No, look . . .'

He'd put the phone down. I stood back, annoyed and yet wondering how he managed to push my buttons without apparent effort. Just to hear his voice and the way he spoke to me had me completely off balance, genuinely angry at his behaviour and yet with my stomach fluttering for the very same reason, and for the memories of what we'd done. He was coming anyway, and I was still in my robe with my hair like a bird's nest.

As I ran upstairs I was telling myself not to go out of my way for him, but that didn't stop me sorting myself out in record time and slipping into a red summer dress and sandals. He had obviously called from nearby, so arrogant he'd driven over from wherever he lived in the certainty that I'd be free to go off with him, and I could only assume he'd got my number and address from Edward Davis-Brown.

I was still upstairs when the sleek silver Jaguar eased itself into my driveway. It occurred to me to make him wait, but not for long. With my luck Sarah would turn up, or worse, Robert. I ran downstairs instead, composing myself only as I opened the front door, to find him leaning nonchalantly against the bonnet of his car, looking up at my house, then at me.

'Very nice, especially the way it shows off your breasts.'

'Miles, for goodness sake!'

He laughed, making me blush. After what we'd done there was little point in hiding my feelings, but the urge to slap his face was still strong. I climbed into the car, eager to leave, which he noticed and inevitably misinterpreted.

'My, you are keen, but I was thinking of lunch first.'

'Just drive, please. Where have you come from, by the way?'

'London.'

'You drove all the way from London on the off chance that I'd be in?'

'No, I spoke to your lodger yesterday afternoon.'

'She didn't say anything.'

'I'm here now.'

I didn't reply immediately as he was concentrating on reversing out of my driveway. Tiggy had presumably forgotten, no doubt easy enough to do after an evening with Saul and his friends. Miles turned left, towards the bypass.

'Where are we going, did you say?'

'The Fattened Goose in Southwold, which is why I don't have time to tie you up like a trussed chicken and fuck your brains out.'

I made to answer, but I knew he'd only laugh. With him there would be no reserve. He knew.

For a while we drove in silence, Miles wearing a quiet little smirk, me trying to come to terms with my own feelings, acutely aware of his lack of respect yet wanting what he could do for me with an urgency that bordered on physical pain. When he reached the bypass he turned east, accelerating hard enough to push me back into my seat as we joined the traffic and quickly reaching ninety with a sublime indifference to fuel consumption, pollutants and the law. I wanted to say something, but everything I could think of seemed trivial, and everything that wasn't trivial I couldn't bring myself to say. He obviously had no such concerns.

'How far does your vegetarian kick extend? I ask because the lobster there is exceptional. They have a holding pot in the river, and—'

'Miles, please, anything, but not that. I don't eat meat, full stop, of any species. Could we talk about something else?'

'Suit yourself. I'm sorry you left so early the other day. I would have liked to show you around Cambridge.'

'I had to get back.'

'Shame. Still, it was good of you not to wake me up. I need my sleep after a dinner like that, to say nothing of pudding.'

His voice held not the slightest hint of concern. Evidently the possibility that I might have wanted to avoid talking to him or never want to see him again simply hadn't crossed his mind. I also understood what he meant by pudding, and it was hardly flattering.

'Do you know something, I'd have put a thousand pounds against you coming in to my room.'

'Oh? I thought you were expecting me?'

'Far from it.'

'You did ask.'

'Yes, but I didn't expect you to accept, never mind like that! It really took me by surprise, I can tell you.'

I found myself smiling with a trace of pride as I remembered how I'd wanted to show him I wasn't the cold fish he imagined.

'So you didn't think I'd accept at all, at first that is?'

'No, I didn't. The truth is I'd marked you down as a bit of a virago. I only made the offer to prick your superiority.'

'Me, superior?'

'Absolutely. It's your reputation, after all.'

'My reputation? With whom?'

'My industry for a start, which is one reason we want you on board.'

'I'm not for sale. This isn't about that job, is it?'

'Oh no, this is personal.'

'Good.'

With that word I'd more or less admitted I was willing, and his smirk grew a trifle broader. Then he put his foot down more firmly, leaving me clutching the seat as he shot past a lorry as if it was at a standstill. Occasionally I'd imagined being driven in a large, fast car as an element of my fantasies, but the reality was terrifying and made worse by his nonchalance.

'Would you mind not driving quite so fast?' I asked, with a trace of irritation to my voice.

He slowed marginally, leaving me to think over how he saw me, or rather, how he had seen me before. Whatever the situation, presenting reports on industry and the environment, protesting in a dozen ways, holding my place on picket lines, I'd always assumed my opponents looked on me as no more than a nuisance, and inherently weak. In fact it had often been the sense that I was of little or no consequence that had driven me to try my hardest, and had no doubt contributed to a good many victories. To learn that an executive with MacDouglas Alpha regarded me as a virago and as superior was enormously satisfying. It also made it a great deal easier to express my sexuality with him, knowing that his brash exterior was largely defensive and that I really had taken him by surprise.

I closed my eyes to shut out the view of the countryside moving past my window at alarming speed and relaxed, imagining how it might be if we could be completely honest with each other, each of us taking pleasure in what had been mutual antagonism. For him it would be taking out his frustrations on my body, for me, allowing him to do so and thereby fulfilling all my deepest, darkest needs.

Maybe I couldn't admit to our affair, which seemed to be what was starting, but that was purely a private decision, not an ethical one. Knowing that what we did together was secret would also add to the pleasure immensely, and with luck it would help me put my feelings for Tiggy out of my mind. After all, he now seemed likely to provide precisely what I craved from her.

The restaurant was not the nightmare I had expected it to be, and Miles was even moderately considerate about his choice of food. He was also careful about the amount of wine he drank but insisted on making appropriate choices for each course, which meant that by the time we left Southwold I had drunk the best part of two bottles and was feeling extremely mellow, also aroused in a sleepy kind of way. I wanted him to stop in some convenient lay-by and take me into the woods, tie my hands with bailer twine and thoroughly enjoy himself with me.

I asked, but he said he had something better in mind, driving at breakneck speed back across Suffolk. Whatever it was, it had to be good, with his knack of knowing exactly what would bring me the most pleasure without ever having to ask. It was late afternoon by the time we got back, and to my great relief Tiggy was still out. I knew that she was unlikely to be back until late, leaving plenty of time. Miles glanced around as he closed the door behind him.

'Are we alone?'

'Yes, but put the lock on.'

He nodded and slid the catch into place with a deliciously final click as he gave me my first instruction.

'Bedroom, Hazel, now.'

There was no need to be coy, no need to hesitate. I went straight to the stairs, Miles following with his eyes fixed firmly to me as I climbed. As he entered my bedroom he closed the door behind him and glanced around, smiling as he saw my robe on the back of the door, the same one I had worn to come to him before.

'Put your hands behind your back, Hazel.'

I obeyed, my body shivering with anticipation as I turned my back to him and crossed my wrists, offering myself for bondage. He pulled the cord free and stepped close, his fingers strong and assured as he twisted the cord into place, once more bringing me the exquisite sensation of being rendered helpless. As he tied the knot off my control had simply vanished, both mentally and physically. He could do as he pleased with me and I would just lap it up.

'Now then, what shall I do with you? Hmm ... yes, why not. Do you have a scarf or something like that?'

'What for?'

He immediately planted a firm smack on my bottom, leaving my flesh tingling as he went on.

'Don't ask questions, Hazel, just do as you're told. I'm going to blindfold you, that's all. Do you have a scarf?'

'Yes, in my top drawer, on the left.'

Despite the position I was in there was a touch of embarrassment as he pulled open my knicker drawer, and rather more as he made a quick inspection of the contents before withdrawing a red silk scarf I'd been given by Robert at Christmas. Miles folded it twice and stepped back to me, placing it across my face and my view of him was replaced by dull red nothingness. As he knotted it off behind my head my shaking was growing harder, my sense of helplessness stronger, and stronger still as he began to explore my body, touching through my dress, but wherever he pleased. His voice was calm and amused as he took my breasts in his hands.

'Nice, full and heavy without being overblown, firm too.'

As he finished his fingers closed on my nipples,

pulling at them to make me gasp and stumble for-
wards a little. He chuckled and let go, only to continue
his exploration, stroking me with his fingertips, across
my breasts, down over my belly and hips, tracing the
curve of my bottom as he went behind me. Just his
touch was enough to bring me so high I already
wanted to come, and yet he didn't seem to be hurried
at all, enjoying my helplessness at leisure until at last
he stepped away.

'Hmm, yes, that will add a nice touch, yes . . .'

He didn't finish, and I was left standing, tied and
blindfolded, not daring to move. It was impossible to
make out what he was doing, beyond the occasional
faint click, but I knew it involved me, and intimately.
When he'd finished he came back, touching me once
more, ruffling my hair and tracing a slow line from the
nape of my neck down my back to my bound hands
and lower still, exploring the contours of my bottom
with a casually intimacy that had me gasping before
he took his hand away and spoke.

'Very nice, very nice indeed, and with such a nice
bottom there's only one thing to be done.'

'What's that?'

'I'm going to spank you.'

'Spank me?'

'Yes, Hazel, spank you. I'm going to turn you over
my knee, take down your knickers and spank you. How
about that?'

'I . . . I don't know!'

'Oh, I think you'll like it. I've yet to meet a woman
who doesn't, only something tells me you might be a
bit precious about it, so we're going to play a little
game.'

He was right. The thought of what he'd threatened
to do filled me with an inexpressible outrage. It was

just plain wrong, an utterly unacceptable thing to do to a woman, something no man had the right to do, not ever. Only Miles was going to do it to me, and the threat had set my stomach fluttering uncontrollably and made my knees so weak I could barely stand. The blood had come up to my face and chest too, and he saw, chuckling in satisfaction as the strength of my reaction made itself obvious.

'You are in a state, aren't you. Is this your first time?'

I nodded urgently, astonished that he should think for a moment that anybody else, ever, might have done such an outrageous thing to me.

'Excellent! This I am going to enjoy. Now, you will do just as I say. First, tell me what I'm going to do to you.'

I couldn't, at first. The words stuck in my throat, and when I did manage they came out as a faint mumble.

'You . . . you're going to spank me.'

He laughed.

'You can do better than that, Hazel. Come on, nice and clear.'

Again I tried, forcing myself to obey him, but barely able to believe it was my own voice as I spoke.

'You are going to spank me.'

'Good, that's better, but I want a little more detail. What did I say, exactly?'

I knew. The words were still burning in my mind, but again it was hard to get them out.

'You . . . you bastard! You're . . . ow!'

He'd smacked my bottom, really quite hard, enough to sting and bring my passion to the point at which I was gasping for breath as he gave a tut of mock disapproval.

'Language, Hazel, really. Now we're going to do it again, properly this time. On the count of three, you will tell me what I am going to do to you, in detail, and how much you'll enjoy it. One. Two. Three.'

I swallowed hard, my mouth working but no sound coming out, until suddenly I'd found my voice, thick with emotion as I said the awful words.

'You're going to spank me. You're going to turn me over your knee and take down my knickers and spank me.'

'What am I going to spank, Hazel?'

'My bottom.'

'Say it, properly.'

'Yes, Miles. You're going to turn me over your knee and take down my knickers and spank my bottom.'

'That's better. One more time for Daddy.'

'Oh God ... You ... you're going to turn me over your knee and take down my knickers and spank my bottom. Yes. Yes, please do it, Miles. Do it now, you bastard. Spank me. Spank me really hard, really, really hard!'

He just laughed and took hold of my arm, steering me gently but firmly to the bed. I let him do it, close to tears as I was pulled down, not of distress, but of raw, overpowering emotion. He was really going to do it, to spank my bottom, just the way he had threatened, and with my hands tied. It was too much, but that didn't matter. I was helpless, and that did. Over I went, laid across his knees with my hips pushed up, a position that brought me an overwhelming sense of shame, yet was powerfully erotic.

My mouth had come open of its own accord, my eyes were shut behind my blindfold, all my senses focused on what was being done to me as he got me ready, my dress slowly lifted up my back, my knickers taken down with a single, purposeful movement, one leg curled around mine to ensure that I couldn't even struggle properly. I was shaking hard and biting my lip, expecting the pain of a slap at any moment, but when his hand did touch me it was gentle, the palm laid softly across my trembling cheeks. As he began to caress me he spoke.

'This is how you should be, Hazel, down across my knee with your lovely full bottom pushed up, ready for the first spanking of your life, and so well deserved. Tell me you need it, one more time.'

I was talking immediately, too far gone to hold back.

'I need it, Miles, I really need it. Now spank me hard. Punish me. Put me in my place.'

He gave a brief, knowing chuckle, his hand lifted and came back down, a single firm swat and I was being spanked. It was hard, and it stung, but just that first smack sent a jolt of pleasure through me, and as the second followed and the third, I'd lost control of myself completely, pushing my bottom up in abandoned ecstasy and begging him to do it harder. He obliged, to set me gasping across his legs, my arms jerking in my bonds.

It was perfect, exactly what I'd wanted – my hands tied behind my back as a strong, dominant male spanked my bare bottom. Shivers of ecstasy were running through me with every smack and I could feel myself growing hot behind, with a warm, fulfilling glow that spread out from my bottom to the rest of my body, creating a sense of sexual need beyond even what I'd experienced with my hands tied.

When his cupped hand slipped down between my open thighs I no longer even felt ashamed. I opened my legs for him, and as he began to manipulate me the spanking began again with his other hand, harder still and punctuated by the occasional tug on my bound wrists just to remind me how helpless I was. He was growing excited too, his cock pressing into my side, and as I thought of where he was about to put it my orgasm hit me.

I would soon be over the bed with my hands still tied and my bottom red with spanking, a position so deliciously undignified in which to be taken, to be fucked. I'd be helpless, bare to him, wet and ready from my climax, his to enjoy just as he pleased.

My cry of ecstasy rang loud in the room as I came, not one time, but again and again in succession, hitting a new peak with every smack of his hand on my now blazing bottom. I only stopped when he did, and was left gasping for breath and shaking uncontrollably, also still desperately in need for his cock, which was just as well.

He was no longer calm, but urgent and full of passion as he hauled me quickly around and into a kneeling position by the bed. I heard the rasp of his zip, his hand twisted into my hair and he had fed his cock into my mouth, making me suck him without as much as bothering to ask, just as I had imagined men doing so many times. I thought he would come, he was so urgent, but after only a moment he had pulled back.

A single push and I was down over the bed, my bottom pushed out to him as he scrambled round behind me. I felt him touch me, and slide deep in, setting me gasping once more as he took a firm grip on my hips. He began to fuck me, firm, even thrusts that pushed his body against me every time, faster and faster still, only to stop. I heard my own moan of disappointment as he pulled back, then his voice.

'Don't worry, I'm not done with you yet. First, let's have those fine titties out.'

He took hold of my dress, pushing it up until it was rucked around my back and my breasts were free, and in his hands as he cupped them, his cock now a rigid bar between the cheeks of my bottom. Again I thought he would come, just as he was, taking full enjoyment of me, but as he pulled back a little he spoke again.

'And now, Dr Hazel Jones, I am going to sodomise you.'

Even as he spoke he had pushed himself between my cheeks. My stomach went tight, I tried to protest, but all that came out was a broken sob and I was pushing myself out to meet him, my final shred of reservation overcome by my desperate need. He went in, right in, deep up my well-smacked bottom, tightened his grip on my breasts, and began to pump.

I just came, from nowhere, overcome by what was being done, screaming and begging for more as the scene played over and over in my head: me, tied up, blindfolded, spanked, brought off under his fingers, fucked and finally, for the first time in my life, sodomised.

12

Once again I found myself asking what I'd done, and once again I found that the pleasure far outweighed any cost. Miles cared very little if our relationship was open or not, but the idea of my having to keep it secret from my friends amused him, while I made it very clear that the situation was not negotiable.

One person did find out, Tiggy, although she of course had no idea who he was and wouldn't have minded in any case. She came back while we were still in the shower, much earlier than I'd have expected, and it was quite plain what we'd been up to, although fortunately not in detail. Her reaction was typical, easy acceptance, at least on the surface, but as the three of us sat drinking coffee together after Miles and I had dressed I was sure I could see hurt in her eyes and hear it in the tone of her voice.

Despite what he and I had just done it didn't stop his eyes wandering to her chest and legs, which I suppose was only to be expected, but raised conflicting emotions in me, jealousy and a hot, piquant curiosity for how it would be for the three of us to have sex together. Not that it was possible, anymore than between just Tiggy and I, and even in all his arrogance it didn't seem to occur to Miles, who got up from the table as soon as he'd finished his coffee.

'It's been a long day, Hazel, a great one, but a long one. I should be getting back.'

'OK. Will I see you soon?'

'I'll call.'

He bent to kiss me and I followed him to the door, opening it to reveal his Jaguar, something that was sure to raise eyebrows if he came to visit regularly.

'Do you have another car?'

'Yes, a BMW Z4.'

'Oh, never mind. Call me soon, yes?'

I reached up to kiss him and his arms came around me, first in a hug, and then with a meaningful double pat to my bottom.

'I will. Oh, and I've left a little present for you.'

'You have? What is it?'

'You'll find out.'

He broke away as he spoke, kissed me one last time and turned for the car. I watched him go, full of an emotion I hadn't felt so strongly since I was a teenager, and I was smiling as I walked back into the house. Tiggy wasted no time.

'Who's he, if you don't mind me asking?'

'Not at all. He's called Miles.'

'He's gorgeous!'

She meant it, but again there was that hint in her voice. I shrugged, wishing I could talk to her to explain how things stood, but completely unable to do so. It was an awkward situation to say the least, especially as her reaction showed a fragility which appealed to me in the same way as had Miles's admission that he considered me something of a virago. Both represented something of the establishment that filled me with such ambivalent feelings, but underneath both were as human as me. The only thing I could think of was to try and cheer her up some other way.

'If you're not doing anything we could go to the Artichoke? My treat.'

'Thanks for the offer, but Saul's coming for me later. So is Dean, and I think they're hoping you'll come out riding, but really I'd rather come to –'

My phone rang and Tiggy went quiet as I answered it.

'Hazel? Sarah. We've got problems down at The Cottage. Robert won't do it this evening. He says he'd got crossed wires but it's really 'cause he can't handle the gay guys. He can be such a prat sometimes. Could you do it?'

'Me? I don't know, Sarah.'

'Please, Hazel, I really need this.'

'Couldn't one of their staff do it or something?'

'That's the whole point, Hazel, we need somebody other than a gay male to show solidarity with their community.'

'Um . . . oh, OK, but not too late.'

'Just until closing time. The police are likely to turn up to see what's going on, maybe even somebody from the council, so it's vital we have a presence. Thanks, Hazel, I knew you'd be up for it.'

She rang off, doubtless in order to persuade somebody else to some other cause. Tiggy was waiting for a reply.

'Don't worry, you go out with Saul and the boys. I've got to sit outside a gay bar and hand out leaflets.'

I thought of Josh as I spoke, but decided not to bring the subject up. After all, she might not have known anything about it. My leaflets were upstairs and I went to collect them, reminding me of Miles's remark about a present as I entered my bedroom. There was nothing obvious, certainly nothing easily identifiable as a present, although he'd done something while I was still blindfolded, so possibly it was hidden somewhere. That meant it was small, and I immediately thought of a ring, only to dismiss the idea as ridiculous when we'd only seen each other twice.

A brief hunt in obvious places such as under my pillow didn't reveal anything, and as I went back downstairs with the leaflets I was wondering if he hadn't been making a joke about the lingering warmth from the spanking he'd given me. Knowing him that was probably it, and I put it to the back of my mind as I got into my coat and set off for town. Saul and Dean passed as I was waiting at the bus stop, but neither saw me in the gathering dusk.

It was dark by the time I got to The Cottage, and very different from my previous visit. Bright lights shone from the interior and there were plenty of men already there and more coming every minute as I took my place. One or two greeted me, most ignored me, while there were few if any other passers-by, leaving me bored and quietly cursing Sarah within half-an-hour of turning up.

The staff was too busy to worry about me either, so there was no beer or coffee on offer. I also began to need the loo. Before long my patience was beginning to wear thin and I decided to go in and get myself something. The moment I was through the door the smell of leather and hot male bodies hit me, but I ignored the surprised or curious looks and pushed my way through to the bar, shouting to the barman above the noise of the music.

'May I have a coffee, please, and I'd like to use your loo.'

He looked doubtful but answered me.

'No coffee this evening. The loo's down the end, but there's no Ladies.'

'Never mind. I'll have a beer then, in a minute.'

There might not have been a Ladies, but there wasn't a choice either. I made my way to the back, far from happy with the situation but glad they were gay as it considerably reduced my embarrassment, until I pushed open the loo door.

Josh was there, squatting down in front of a huge black guy, and the reason he was squatting was that he was sucking his friend's cock. It was quite some cock too, thick and extraordinarily long, fully erect and straining up from the man's open fly and into Josh's mouth. Both had their eyes closed in bliss, and I could only stare, watching as Josh's mouth moved on the huge deep-brown shaft, one man with another man's penis in his mouth.

I knew, of course, the sort of things gay men did, and had even fantasised about watching, but to see gay cocksucking in the flesh, and as an uninvited voyeur, was something else entirely. It set my mouth dry and my stomach fluttering, my imagination immediately running at full speed, but what it didn't do was stop me needing the loo.

'Excuse me, may I just get past. Sorry to disturb you.'

Both of them opened their eyes, but I was already past. The next couple of minutes were among the most embarrassing of my life, but perhaps no more so for them than for me. When I'd finished they were gone, much to my relief, although the image of the black man's enormous erection in Josh's mouth was fixed firmly in my mind and wasn't going away in a hurry.

I went back outside to drink my beer, feeling rather conspicuous and wondering if I should abandon my post and find some excuse for Sarah. Nobody was about except the occasional customer, leaving the alley quiet and rather forbidding. I considered going inside, but my presence evidently made many of them feel uncomfortable. As I wavered between going and staying I was cursing Sarah once more, and when Josh came out I was more grateful than embarrassed. He was wearing a sheepish grin.

'Hello Josh. I'm very sorry about that.'

'No, it was my fault. We shouldn't have been, not with snoops from the council around. Sorry if we embarrassed you.'

'Not at all. It's your bar; you should be allowed to do as you please.'

He gave a pleased grin but didn't reply. I wanted him to stay outside and talk to me, so quickly went on.

'You seem to have a very close community here.'

'Yeah, yeah, I suppose we do.'

'Have you been coming long?'

'Yeah.'

'It must be good to have somewhere dedicated to your own tastes, where you can do as you like without people judging you.'

'Yeah.'

He wasn't being very communicative, but he didn't seem in any hurry to go inside either, squatting down on his heels and putting his beer bottle to his mouth in a manner disturbingly reminiscent of what he'd been doing before. I felt I needed to say something more, and was curious to know about Tiggy and him, so chose my words carefully.

'I think you know one of my students, Tiggy Blackmore?'

'Yeah? What's she look like?'

It wasn't the answer I'd expected.

'A little over average height, very long blonde hair.'

'Oh yeah, I know her, sort of. She used to bring the oranges out at half-time and do the tea after matches and stuff.'

It wasn't at all the answer I'd expected.

'Oh. Didn't you, um . . . weren't you and she together for a while, last year?'

'Me?'

I could see he wanted to laugh at me for making what was quite obviously a ludicrous suggestion.

'I'm sorry, I think there must have been a misunderstanding. Perhaps it was somebody else.'

'Yeah, must've been.'

'You, um . . . you've never been out with a woman at all? Sorry, I don't mean to seem intrusive, only . . .'

I trailed off as he turned to look me full in the face, now grinning, and as I realised what he thought I was trying to say the blood rose in to my face in a hot blush. This time he did laugh.

'No, love, I'm not into that. Boys only, that's me. If you want to watch, there's a couple of guys inside who might be up for it?'

My cheeks were blazing as I stammered out a refusal, but he went on.

'That's cool, we get plenty of fag hags around. What, did watching me suck on Roland's prick get to you? Big, isn't he?'

I was still struggling to find a reply when Roland himself came out. He gave me a look, and not a very friendly one, before jerking his thumb back towards the door. Josh went in, not even pausing to say goodbye, and Roland followed, leaving me on my own once more. If I'd ever felt more embarrassed I couldn't remember when, and I decided I'd had enough.

In due course I knew I'd be thinking about what Josh had offered me in a very different way, perhaps even regretting not having accepted his offer, but as I waited for a taxi to take me home that wasn't what was on my mind. Either he had lied, or Tiggy had. I wanted to know which, but there was no obvious answer. Josh was clearly the passive partner in his relationship to Roland, and might well have wanted to deny ever having had straight interests, perhaps even to himself. I couldn't think of any reason for Tiggy to do so, and yet that wasn't the only thing that didn't add up.

Her ability to do as she pleased was pretty extraordinary, as if she led a charmed life. She did, or at least she seemed to, but to manage at least one sexual encounter every single day for five months was surely asking a bit much. On reflection, so were some of the details, especially all the times she'd had it outdoors, right from the beginning. Even allowing for global warming going stark naked outdoors at the beginning of January was pushing it, either sitting on a car bonnet to be licked or riding a motorbike. It wasn't impossible, just improbable, yet when I considered all the improbable events in sequence, the probability of everything being true became very low indeed.

Maybe there was more to the entries than met the eye? I'd already considered the possibility that she used her diary as a form of catharsis, in substitute for the confessions she no longer attended. Yet it had to be more than that, because I knew that at least some of the details were true, the non-sexual ones at least. Then there was the lack of the sort of mundane detail most people would have filled their diaries with.

I had finished *The Poor Mouth*, which led to me thinking about the distinction between truth, perceived truth and outright lies. The early part of the book was realistic, with no more exaggeration than was needed to make it amusing and maintain the parody. Only when Bonaparte was chased by the Sea Cat did the story leave the realms of the possible, and even that could easily be put down to night fears. Impossible it might be, but it was also very human.

Then came the incident with Maeldoon O'Poenassa, which began realistically enough, but was obviously a fabrication from the point at which he discovered the spring of whisky and the old man began to talk to him. With that, the story had taken on a new level, because it became possible that the narrative was no longer merely exaggerated, but entirely false, and designed to explain away the twenty golden pennies, not to the peelers, but to the reader. Thus, by the end of the book it was impossible to decide if Bonaparte was the innocent victim of the cruel and arbitrary English justice system imposed on the hapless Gaels, or a murderer.

Critics disagreed on O'Brien's intentions, and it struck me as more likely that the question had been left deliberately open. Possibly Tiggy was doing something similar, using her diary in a complicated way, not merely to record her life, but her desires as well, blurring the lines between fact and fantasy for the sake of her own emotional state. In that case her telling me she'd been out with Josh might be part of the same thing, the expression of an unfulfilled desire as fact made in order to cope with her emotions, just as I did by evolving complicated fantasies to enhance my orgasms.

I knew I would have to look at her diary again, assuming she wasn't back from her jaunt with Saul, and she wasn't. This time there was only limited guilt. I felt I needed to know if she'd lied to me, and how that related to her supposed feelings for me. Not that it was necessarily easy to be sure, and as I sat down at her desk and carefully opened the familiar blue book I was thinking as a scientist and not in terms of erotic fantasy.

My initial aim was to find an outright lie, something that was not only improbable, but impossible. The weekend she'd been to visit her parents and taken me to the Artichoke seemed a strong possibility, and I flicked through until I found it.

April 23rd Sunday

Roast beef for lunch and Kiyoshi for afters while Mum did the washing up and Dad snoozed on the sofa. Felt great doing it and knowing we might get caught, especially from behind. Imagine being caught like that!

Back to Keynes later. Went to a restaurant and talked art with X.

It was as brief as always, and accurate. I tried another one.

May 6th Saturday

Had to get back to Brancaster double quick for X. Saul was a bastard about it and made me pay him off by putting it up my bum.

Walked on the beach with X. Oh, I wish!

It was odd, because she'd already been in Brancaster that morning, with Saul. He'd only had to drive her half a mile down to the beach car park, hardly reason for her to allow herself to do anything if she didn't want to, let alone that. It looked very like fantasy, but I couldn't be sure. I began to turn the pages at random, hoping to find something better. It didn't take long.

May 11th Thursday

Tutorial day and I'm in trouble, nice trouble. X says my assignment's useless. I told her I'm a bad, lazy girl and she should smack my bottom for me, so she did. She made me bend over her desk and told me to lift my skirt, but she took my knickers down herself. Just being bare in front of her felt so good I nearly came, and when she smacked me and told me off I did. So good!

I read it again, and again, my mouth hanging open. It was pure fantasy, and couched in the language of fantasy, some of it almost word for word with what Miles had made me say before my own spanking. Yet not a word of it was true. Worse, the mere accusation would have been enough to have me suspended immediately, even sacked.

Now I had to talk to her.

The problem was, what to say? The situation had become abruptly serious, and also complicated. My discovery had made her seem less perfect, more human, but also less predictable. If I confessed to reading her diary the consequences might be disastrous, and I simply could not allow something so dangerous to my career to go unchallenged.

Her reasons for writing what she had were too deep for me to fathom, but I felt I could safely dismiss the possibility that it had been done as some sort of complicated attempt at blackmail. Leaving aside her lack of motive, it was too elaborate. More probably it was genuinely what she wanted from me, and not so very different to what I wanted from her, only I wished that like me she had had the sense to keep it in her head.

All I could think of was to bring up a similar subject and make a joke of how risky such behaviour would be, hopefully making her realise her mistake and so destroy the evidence. That assumed she was genuinely fond of me, but that at least I was sure I could guarantee. She had never been anything but friendly, and her desire for discipline from me was plainly linked to pleasure.

I didn't want to talk to her until I'd made a firm decision, so put the diary carefully back on top of the big stack of journals were she'd left it and went to bed. Over two hours later I was still awake and I heard the motorbikes come back, then the door as she let herself in. As usual she called my name softly to see if I was up, but I didn't reply.

There was no time for a serious discussion on the Monday morning, so I behaved as usual, taking a bus into the department together for my nine o'clock lecture. I didn't see her for the rest of the day, as I was with my third years for most of the morning and had a first year practical all afternoon. It involved basic statistics, something they always had difficulty getting to grips with, and by the time I'd finished explaining how T-tests work for the umpteenth time it was gone five o'clock and I was badly in need of a cup of tea. I was still drinking it in the foyer when Tiggy came out of the library, greeting me with the same calm, friendly smile as always. I responded in kind.

'Hello. Are you going back?'

'Yes.'

We fell into step together, as we had done many times before, only now it was harder than ever to keep my voice level.

'Are you busy this evening?'

'No, not at all. Gareth said he might come round, but...'

She left the sentence unfinished with a small shrug of indifference.

'You mentioned The Artichoke yesterday, and I thought it might be nice to go?'

'Yeah, great.'

'We could go straight there, if you like, perhaps have a drink first if they're not open. You can leave your books in my room.'

'OK.'

The Artichoke was open, and half-an-hour later we were seated at a table outside, sipping chilled white wine as I tried to work out exactly what I should say and Tiggy chatted blithely about the night before.

'I'd have far rather have come out with you. Saul's OK, but this jealousy thing's getting worse and worse, and he's always push, push, push, you know. Can I ask you something?'

'Of course, anything at all.'

'OK, thanks. What would you do if you just want to be friends with somebody, but they're making a real issue about sex, and asking for stuff you didn't want to give?'

'Explain the situation and point out that he had no right to make that sort of demand, I imagine. I can see it would be very difficult to remain friends if he was unwilling to accept that, but then you have to ask yourself if you want to associate with somebody who won't respect your personal limits.'

I was wondering who she was thinking of, as she seemed so sexually active and confident in her actions, to say nothing of the sort of things she liked. Not that all of it was necessarily true, or any of it, but the desire had to be there, surely, just from the way she'd expressed herself. She gave a thoughtful grimace and went on.

'It's tricky. I know it's all because of the way I was brought up, and I ought to shake that off, but I just don't feel ready. I definitely don't want him to be my first, but I can't tell him that, and ... and maybe I was a bit stupid, because last term I did him in my hand because I thought it would shut him up, but it just made him worse. Now I let him ... give him bjs, you know, suck him, but he wants more and he gets more and more jealous. He says I should get over it, that I'm just scared, and keeps going on about Gareth, claiming I let him, which I don't! It's really difficult, and all I ever wanted to do was be friends.'

I couldn't answer immediately, the implications of what she was saying sinking in. She was a virgin, and little more experienced than I'd been at her age; a very different person from the highly promiscuous, super-confident young woman of her diary. Even what she did do with Saul, who was obviously the one she was talking about, seemed reluctant, with none of the open joy she expressed in her private thoughts. Suddenly she seemed fragile, all her poise gone in an instant, and I realised it had never been more than a protective shell. She spoke again.

'What do you think?'

'It's difficult, let me think ... First of all, he has no right whatsoever to put pressure on you. That's wrong of him, and the obvious solution is not to see him any more. I know that's not what you want to do, but I suspect that if you try to find a compromise he'll continue to exert pressure on you.'

'That's for sure!'

'If he won't be reasonable, you have a choice. Either give in, which you should never feel you have to do unless you want to, or break off the relationship. I'm sorry if that sounds harsh, but I really don't see a middle ground.'

'You're right. Why do men have to be like that? I think I'll go and join the lesbian society.'

She'd said it as a joke, but I couldn't help but wonder if she was testing me. I managed a noncommittal smile and hid my face behind the menu as I went on.

'The thing is, Tiggy, that if you let the situation continue you may get to the point where it becomes unpleasant, and then you'll have to put it on a formal basis. Given that you've allowed him oral sex, and that his friends are sure to back him up, you'll be in a weak position. I really do advise ending the relationship. Sorry.'

'You're right. Thank you, Hazel.'

She sounded close to tears, and I couldn't help but reaching a hand out to give hers a reassuring squeeze. I also saw my chance to get my point across.

'That sort of situation really is best avoided, if you can possibly help it. Yes, there comes a point at which it's your duty to make a complaint, but it's much better not to get to that point in the first place. If the case isn't clear cut and it gets to court it can be extremely distressing. For instance, anything you'd said, you'd written down, letters, emails, anything, might well be used in court in an effort to discredit you as a witness. Personally I never put anything in writing if it could possibly be misconstrued, or cause difficulty if things change. I'd advise you to do the same.'

She'd been listening intently, and nodded her agreement. Hopefully I'd said enough. The waiter had come, and we took a moment to put our order together, but the moment he was out of earshot Tiggy started to talk again.

'You seem to cope so well.'

'Do I?'

'Yes. You'd been with Robert for quite a bit, hadn't you, and then he goes off with your best friend. I'd have been devastated.'

'It did hurt, but not as much as it might have done. Things weren't going too well with Robert anyway, and I really think our relationship had run its course. We weren't committed to each other, although I won't pretend to be happy about finding out he'd been with Eve.'

'Had he?'

'I'm not sure. Maybe not. He wasn't for me anyway.'

'No? He seems very nice.'

'He is, too nice, and not very exciting.'

'And Miles? You don't mind me asking, do you?'

'No. It's good to have somebody I can talk to.'

It was, for all the complications surrounding us, and with the wine slowly soothing away my reservations I wondered if I could tell her rather more. After all, what she'd written might not be true, but it had to say a lot about her needs and I'd never met anyone else who came as close to sharing my feelings. I went on, guarded, but only so much.

'Miles is different. I ought to hate him, but he does something for me no other man ever has, and so naturally. Robert always had to be told, or he'd always ask my permission. Miles seems to know what to do, almost by instinct, even things I've never really thought about.'

I stopped, thinking of how it would feel to have her treat me the way he did, especially the spanking, a taste Tiggy evidently shared. Yet it was too much, too intimate. I took a swallow of wine, hoping the hot blush that had risen to my face wasn't obvious as Tiggy went on.

'I think I understand. It's a bit like that with Saul,

and this Japanese guy called Kiyoshi I see at home. They're fun to be with, exciting, but not easy to just talk to, or relax with.'

'But you don't feel ready in any case?'

'No, but it's more than that. They're too crude. I'm sure they couldn't give me what I really want. I don't think they'd even understand.'

'That was part of my problem with Robert. He wasn't prepared to go outside his own frame of reference.'

'How do you mean?'

'Sex wise. He ... he wants to be understanding, caring, tolerant, but there was never much real feeling. It was as if he only did things because he thought he should, but when it came to something different, something outside current liberal conventions, he couldn't cope at all.'

I'd very nearly told her, but a couple had paused to greet each other beside where we were sitting and I wasn't about to broadcast my love of bondage to the entire town. Tiggy gave a sigh.

'I know, men are like that, anything different and they think you're weird. It can never just be fun, either; it always has to be a big deal. And they say it's women who're always after commitment. The truth is, they want commitment from us to them, but want to play around themselves.'

'I'm afraid that's often the way although, to be fair, you are very attractive, and if you do ... little things, men are sure to want more.'

'Why? I don't mind what I do with Saul, but he won't give the same in return, he just wants me to go further while he won't budge an inch. It's not like I tease him and then let him down.'

'I think it's that men tend to see sex in terms of

goals. It shows in the language, as in "how far did you get", or there's an American phrase, from baseball I think, "I didn't get past first base". Full sex is generally the ultimate goal, and therefore even though you satisfy Saul physically you haven't satisfied his ego.'

The waiter had brought out our starters, a salad of avocado pears and nuts for me, and for a while we ate in silence. Our bottle was empty and I ordered another, now wanting to open up to her more than ever and sure a few more glasses would help. So far I might have had much the same conversation with Eve, if perhaps not Sarah, and yet I knew Tiggy would understand things neither of them would be able to cope with. I would have to be careful not to let it go too far, but just as I would have hoped she could explain things to Saul, so I now could to her.

A group of students came to sit at the table beside us, limiting our conversation until they had finished their coffees and moved on. By then our second bottle was nearly finished and we were eating our main courses, while we'd talked about everything from absinthe to zooplankton, the first of which led back to what was really on my mind.

'Did you ever see *Irma la Douce*?'

'No, I don't think so. Is it a film?'

'Yes, but adapted from a French musical. It's quite clever, I think, with a good balance between comedy and tragedy. It deals with absinthe drinking too, which was a serious problem in Paris before it was banned.'

'But it's legal here?'

'I've seen it in shops, so I suppose it must be. Anyway, the plot deals with a man who forms a relationship with a prostitute but can't bear to think of her having sex with other men. He sets himself as her sole client, pretending he only wants to talk to her, but it becomes so expensive he has to kill off his *alter ego*, and so he gets charged with murdering himself.'

'That's a nice twist.'

'It works out in the end, and it's an interesting take on jealousy, with a man who'd be prepared to alter his entire life in order to prevent his partner having sex with other men, even though he's always known she's a prostitute. So if you think Saul's bad . . .'

'Oh, I can just see him doing that. I can see him as a pimp anyway.'

'That's a bit unfair, isn't it?'

'I don't think so. That lot have no respect for anybody.'

I nodded, remembering how they'd planned to leave me on the heath in the middle of the night for a joke. Tiggy was drunk, her eyes bright and wide, her conversation unguarded. I felt much the same.

'Maybe you're right. I'm sure they told you all about what happened . . .'

I left my sentence open, unsure of myself, and of her reaction. Her reply was equally cautious.

'They said something, but they're always boasting. I know you went riding with them.'

'What did they say? Tell me, I don't mind.'

She was blushing and trying to suppress her giggles as she replied.

'That you went with Dean first, then Steve and Rick too? They said you did everything, went all the way, with all three of them! Outrageous or what?'

'Do you think it's outrageous'

'To say that? Yes!'

'Do you think they'd really do that?'

'If anyone gave them the chance, sure.'

I couldn't bring myself to admit it, but I couldn't help smiling either. Tiggy very slowly put her glass down on the table as her mouth came open and her eyes grew wide. Suddenly I knew I'd gone too far, but as a wave of shame and embarrassment flooded through me she was already talking.

'It was true? What they said, that you ... you gave them bjs and ... let them do you doggy fashion?'

I was too embarrassed even to reply, or to look at her, and could only make vague gestures with my hands, trying to play down what I'd done as she went on.

'I couldn't, not ever, but oh I wish, just if I knew they wouldn't make such a big deal out of it afterwards, and boast.'

'You would?'

'I wish. You're so bold, Hazel, so in control.'

'Me, in control? In a way, maybe. It was what I wanted.'

'I know, but oh, to have the guts to do that! And ... and what I heard you say you liked to Eve West, sorry, I know I shouldn't have listened.'

She gave me her brightest smile, and despite my embarrassment I couldn't help smiling back. As I'd guessed, she'd overheard, and she didn't mind. That felt wonderful, yet now it was clear that all the things she'd written down were fantasies, no more, and I realised with a relief as powerful as my disappointment that the same no doubt applied to her feelings for me. Yet I had found a friend, somebody I could really talk to, which was safe, and far more sensible.

We'd finished, and I called for bill, insisting on paying it despite Tiggy's protests. As we left we linked arms, talking casually together as we made our way back towards the High Street, about shoes. I knew she had a huge collection, and many of them designer names, but I'd never realised just how much she was into them.

'...the sweetest little Prada sandals with a fish across the strap.'

'Isn't Prada terrible expensive?'

'Oh, I can usually bully Dad into it.'

'I wish my father had been like that!'

'Dad's always been generous, but I hardly ever saw him when I was little. He used to work abroad, you see, installing desalination plants in the Near East. I suppose I just got spoilt because he felt bad about not being there, and now he's retired he likes to see me have the best of everything.'

'You lucky thing.'

'I suppose I am. Shall we get a bottle for home?'

She had stopped outside an off-licence. I hesitated, but my first lecture was at eleven o'clock.

'OK, that would be nice.'

'My treat, as you paid the bill.'

I didn't protest, given that she seemed to have more disposable income than I did. A long career as a senior engineer in the Middle East had clearly left her father both wealthy and guilty, so eager to lavish money on his daughter. I went to the shelf of white wines, but Tiggy was already at the counter.

'Look, Hazel, they've got that absinthe stuff. Shall we try it?'

'I don't know, it's very potent.'

'Oh come on, it's only a tiny bottle, and we don't have to drink it all anyway.'

I turned to where she was looking, at a small bottle of virulent green liquid on the top shelf.

'I'd be interested to taste it. Did I mention that some of the French impressionists used to consider it a source of inspiration?'

'Yes. A bottle of the absinthe, please.'

The shop assistant passed it down, his expression of

deep boredom lifting only briefly as his eyes flicked across Tiggy's chest. She paid for the absinthe and we left, stepping almost straight onto the bus as it drew up outside. Ten minutes later we were home, Tiggy sat back on the living room sofa as I retrieved two tiny sherry glasses from the corner cabinet. They were dusty, and I went to wash them, coming back to find that Tiggy had kicked her shoes off and put her feet up on the sofa. She already had the absinthe bottle open and was cautiously sniffing the top.

'Are you supposed to make cocktails with it, or what?'

'I don't know. I think you drink it neat. They used to call it the green fairy, so I would suppose so. Stop, that's plenty.'

I'd put the glasses down and she'd filled both, almost to the top. Taking mine, I sniffed gingerly and took a sip. It was smooth and rich, tasting of aniseed and mint and herbs, not so very different from the liqueurs I'd sometimes drunk at family Christmases. Tiggy wasn't particularly impressed.

'It's OK, I suppose, nothing special.'

'It's what it does that matters, be careful.'

'I don't care. I want to get drunk.'

'I don't. I have to work tomorrow, and you should be in lectures. One glass and then bed, I think.'

'Yes, Auntie.'

She took a good-sized sip and relaxed back into the sofa before speaking again.

'It's quite nice really, like liquorice balls.'

'I've never had liquorice balls.'

'No, only the salty sort.'

'Sorry?'

'Only not the chocolate sort; more like strawberry.'

'You've lost me, Tiggy. What are you talking about?'

'You know, you must have heard it – *suck on my chocolate, salty balls* – or whatever, I don't know. The song that guy Chef from South Park did.'

'I still don't understand.'

'It's a cartoon; you must have seen it, with the four stupid-looking kids and this black guy who runs a burger van. He had a song out, called "Chocolate Salty Balls", only Dean and Rick and Steve, they're not black, are they? So it's strawberry ... or something pink ... maybe worms, yes, worms. Why do boys' cocks look like worms? It's so gross!'

'They don't.'

'They do, all pink and wriggly and –'

'Hey, hang on, I understand!'

'Yeah, she got it at last!'

'You cheeky thing!'

'So spank me.'

She shut her eyes as she said it, and poured the rest of her absinthe down her throat before her mouth set in a happy, sleepy smile. Her voice was slurred, but I'd heard what she'd said, loud and clear. She was joking, maybe, and I could answer just for fun.

'I just might do that.'

She purred, catlike, and stretched out, before suddenly flipping herself over.

'Go on then, do it. Do it hard, Hazel, give me a punishment.'

The moment had come, my epiphany. I was staring, my vision a touch hazy but clear enough, as she pushed up her bottom and reached back, lifting her skirt to show off a pair of tiny white knickers stretched taut across her cheeks. Again she spoke, her voice rich and thick with desire.

'Come on, Hazel, smack my bum. You want to, don't you? Please say you want to?'

Only with her last few words did her tone change, as if she was about to burst into tears. I'd been holding back, about to tell her I shouldn't and explain why, but with that I gave in, telling myself it couldn't hurt to give her what she needed so badly, and it was just a spanking, not really sex. That wasn't what my body was telling me as I answered her, trying to imitate the manner Miles had used on me.

'OK, I'll do it. I think you need it.'

Her voice was a moan as she replied, and brimming with arousal.

'Do it then, please, please, please. Spank me, Hazel, spank me hard!'

I swallowed my drink and came forward, searching for the words I hoped would help her fantasy, the words Miles had made me say out loud.

'Right, Tiggy ...'

No, that was wrong. I knew what would really get to her.

'Right, Miss Mary Blackmore, it's time you were punished, so I'm going to take down your knickers and spank your bare bottom.'

Her answer was a choking sob, and to quickly thrust two of the cushions under her tummy, lifting her bottom higher still. I was close enough to touch, my heart hammering and the blood singing in my head as I reached out, to feel the resilience of her flesh, her smooth, cool skin, the taut rim of her knickers, and I'd begun to pull them down.

As her bottom came bare she let out a tiny cry, barely audible but packed full of emotion. There was still doubt in my head, a thin, reedy voice screaming at me to stop, that her need had to come from some awful trauma; that I had to be insane for pulling down a student's knickers for sex – any student, any sex –

never mind to spank a girl. That didn't stop me. Down they came, laying bare the full, golden globes of her bottom. One last pause and I was doing it, smacking her across her bare cheeks as I told her she was a naughty girl and needed to be punished.

'Tiggy, you bad, bad girl. Oh, I should have done this a long time ago, and you should have done it to me too, Tiggy. You have such a beautiful bottom, Tiggy, and I'm really going to spank you, so hard.'

'Please, yes, ow! More, Hazel, harder ... make it hurt!'

I grabbed the hem of her skirt and laid in, the last of my doubts vanishing in the face of her open desire, and my own. She went wild, wriggling and squirming her body in my grip, kicking her legs and tossing her long blonde hair, pushing her bottom up to meet the smacks. I could imagine how she felt, held down and hot behind, her cheeks full of the same warm glow Miles had given me and each smack sending a jolt of ecstasy through her. It had to be as good, or better, because she was begging.

'Please, Hazel, do it really hard, really, really hard. Do it right under my bum ... like that, only harder ... much harder. Hurt me, hazel; spank me hard, so hard ... I deserve it. Punish me. Oh God, I've wanted this so long, Hazel. I love you ... I ...'

Her words broke to gasps as I laid in with all my might, my hand smacking down on the fleshiest part of her bottom, right over her sex. I realised she was coming, and twisted my hand hard in the waistband of her skirt, trapping her bottom as she struggled, kicking into the sofa, screaming out her ecstasy and telling me she loved me over and over again as the smacks of my palm on her flesh rang out around the room, until finally she had gone limp.

I stood back, panting, my whole body trembling. My hand stung like anything, and so it should have done, with her whole bottom a glowing red ball. She made no attempt to cover up, leaving her skirt twisted into its own waistband and her knickers around her thighs as she pulled herself into a sitting position and turned me a happy, satisfied grin. Her voice was warm and sultry as she spoke.

'That was lovely, the best. Now what can I do for you, Hazel?'

'The same,' I managed.

She looked surprised.

'The same? You want a spanking, from me?'

'Yes, why not? And if you could maybe ... maybe tie my hands behind my back.'

'I always thought you would want to be in control, but OK, I'll spank you.'

She patted her lap, suddenly stern, but I knew what I had to have.

'Upstairs, Tiggy, you can tie me with the cord from my robe.'

'You are so bad!'

She was giggling as she jumped to her feet and grabbed the bottle of absinthe from the table. I took the glasses, and she kicked off her knickers and ran up the stairs, her skirt still up to leave her bare red cheeks bouncing behind her. I'd done it; let myself go with her, exactly what I'd said I wouldn't do so, so often. Now it was too late. She was going to tie me and spank me, and I could no more resist the offer than I could my own heartbeat.

As we came into my bedroom I could see that she was far from sure of herself, giggling and shaking badly, but it didn't stop her taking the cord as I pulled it free from my robe. She didn't accept it immediately, but took a pull from the absinthe bottle before she spoke to me.

'How should I do it? Do you have a special way?'

'Any way you want, but I like my hands tied behind my back, please.'

She nodded and her tongue flicked out to moisten her lips.

'Can I have your clothes off?'

'If you like. Anything. You take charge. Punish me, if that's what you like.'

'Yes, but what for?'

'I don't know, anything.'

She hesitated before speaking again.

'Did ... did you read my diary?'

I felt the blood rush to my face and, as I hung my head, it was no act.

'Yes. Sorry.'

'Don't be. I know you did. I did it for you, and left it out so you could see it, because I hoped ... I hoped I'd turn you on, that maybe you'd like me. Silly, I know, but ...'

'I do like you, more than that. I think I love you.'

She didn't answer, but then she already had. Instead we came together, cuddling and kissing with open mouths and pure emotion, as equals, until we finally broke apart. There was laughter in her voice as she spoke again.

'I'm not going to let you off though, if you really want to be punished?'

'Yes, I deserve to be.'

'You do. Off with that top, then. You don't know how many times I've imagined seeing you naked, Hazel, or being put across your knee, and all sorts. Right, come on, you help too.'

There was command in her voice as she spoke, and

her hands had gone to the buttons of my blouse. I did the last few, and shrugged it off as she began to fumble with the button of my skirt. It came, quickly pulled down, and my shaking had grown so hard I couldn't open the catch of my own bra. Tiggy did it, letting my breasts spill into her hands and kissing each as she pushed her thumbs into the waistband of my tights.

My tights and knickers came down together, and off. I was nude, in front of her and completely nude, with her still dressed, her skirt now fallen to cover her bottom. It was right, as I should be for her, stark naked and her fully dressed. I crossed my wrists behind my back, closing my eyes to savour the moment as she tied me, tied me for spanking by Tiggy, Miss Mary Blackmore, who was now going to punish me. As she spoke the plummy, superior touch to her voice was suddenly stronger, making me want to obey her even more as she tugged the cord tight around my wrists.

'There we are, nice and tight. Over the bed with you.'

I went, never thinking to disobey, down on my knees and across the bed, my body vulnerable to her. She came close, standing over me with a wicked smirk on her face, her moment of unease gone now she had me tied. So many times I'd imagined myself in similar positions, bound and helpless at the feet of some cruel, lustful man or woman, and now it was real, everything I'd wanted, and more.

She glanced around the room.

'What am I going to do with you? What am I going to give you, let me see, yes, the hairbrush. I'm going to give you the hairbrush.'

She skipped quickly across the room, to take up my hairbrush from on top of my chest of drawers. I swallowed, wondering if it would hurt a lot, but wanting it all the same, just because it was her doing it to me.

She smacked it on her palm, grinning, and stepped towards me once more, to sit down beside me on the bed and curl one arm around my body. The cool, hard surface of the hairbrush touched my bottom, the gentlest of pats as she spoke.

'You asked for this.'

My mouth came open to reply, but all that came out was a gasp as the hairbrush smacked down across my bottom. It stung, far worse than Miles's hand, and she didn't let up either, holding me firmly around my waist as she spanked me. I was panting and kicking immediately, quite out of control and deeply ashamed of the exhibition I was making of myself to her, a student, and so much younger than me. Not that I wanted her to stop, because it was a fantasy come true, being tied up and spanked in the nude by a rich girl little more than half my age.

She just laughed, thoroughly enjoying herself and making my feelings stronger still, the hairbrush smacking down on my cheeks faster and harder. I'd begun to cry out in my pain, but the glorious warm feeling Miles had made me feel was already spreading through me and, before I really knew it, I was pushing up my cheeks and begging for more, just as Tiggy had. I got it, furiously hard and right over my sex, bringing me higher and higher still, to the edge of orgasm, but no further, and I was babbling for what I needed.

'Touch me. I need you to touch me, please, but don't stop.'

Tiggy gave a delighted, drunken giggle and she'd changed her position, kneeling behind me on the floor, her hand between my thighs as she belaboured my bottom with the brush. The instant she touched me I was there, in perfect ecstasy as the image of what she'd done to me rose up in my mind. I had been made to strip naked, tied up and spanked with a hairbrush, masturbated to make me come. She was giggling harder than ever as I came down from my orgasm. The spanking had stopped, but my whole bottom seemed to be on fire as I thanked her. She reached out to stroke my hot skin as she responded.

'Good. I'm glad you liked it. Now I'm going to kiss you better.'

I turned my head, expecting her to come up on the bed, knowing what would happen and that I could not possibly resist. She didn't, staying as she was but leaning forward to kiss me gently on each cheek of my bottom. Then, to my surprise and astonishment and delight her lips pressed to my bottom hole, so rude, and so nice. A moment later she'd pulled the cord around my wrists loose and as I turned she was peeling off her bra and top. Her skirt followed, and like me she was naked.

There was no longer any question of what was going to happen; we were going to bed together. We tumbled in, laughing as she poured out the absinthe into our glasses, clumsily, a little of the thick green liquid splashing onto my chest. Her mouth found me immediately, licking up the spilt drink, kissing too, and taking my nipple into her mouth to suckle on me, her head cradled in my arm, her eyes shut in ecstasy. At last she pulled free, her eyes bright with mischief as they met mine, her mouth open and moist. She raised her glass.

'I want you, Hazel. To us, yes?'

I clinked my glass to hers and swallowed the contents as her hand snaked down over my belly. My thighs came wide by instinct and she was touching me, her fingers burrowing deep as our mouths met in an absinthe-flavoured kiss. That was it, too much to let me hold back, and too late anyway. We rolled into each other's arms, lost to everything except the pleasure of each other's bodies. We were kissing with our mouths open together as our fingers stroked and caressed; sucking, both trying to get at each other's breasts at the same time so that we knocked our heads together and ended up in a giggling heap.

Tiggy bounced up first and twisted around to climb on top of me. I was licking her immediately as we went head to tail, our tongues probing into every secret crevice, lapping with the urgency of fast-approaching climaxes. We came together, our heads locked between each other's thighs, and a third time, later, in a laughing, drunken tangle on the bed. Even then we weren't finished, now completely uninhibited as we let out all our pent-up feelings for each other, still kissing even as I finally lost my senses.

13

This time I really had done it – not only been to bed with one of my own students but another woman as well, to say nothing of the details. Despite that, and the sure knowledge that if what had happened ever came out it would be the end of my job and my career, I found it impossible to feel bad about it. Instead I was singing, so elated I couldn't stop grinning.

Rationally, I knew I'd done something really stupid, and that I should bring it to a close as quickly and with as little damage to both Tiggy and myself as I possibly could. Emotionally, I knew that I was in love with her, my feelings far beyond what I felt for Miles, or had ever felt for Robert. It was very easy to convince myself that telling her it could never happen again was the wrong thing to do, and that only by being together in a secret and trusting relationship could we hope to get through.

In the morning we were both in denial, happy to be with each other, but avoiding any real discussion of what we'd done, and especially the ruder details. Not that I felt any guilt for my behaviour, only the social implications, and Tiggy only hinted at it by blaming the absinthe, something I didn't trouble to deny. If she needed an excuse, then she was welcome to it. Nor did we talk about the possible consequences of what we'd done, but simply had a late breakfast and went into the labs together, her smile as we parted the only evidence of our guilty secret.

The rest of the day passed easily enough, despite my exhaustion and a slightly bad head. Fortunately the entire afternoon was taken up with a third year practical and the students were quite capable of working out oxygen levels in their soil samples with no more than an occasional word of advice from me. I came out promising myself an early night, although I knew full well I'd be sharing my bed with the elegant blonde girl who was waiting for me by the doors.

It was completely normal, something she did most days, as was riding back together on the bus. This time it felt different, as if Big Brother himself was watching our every move though the CCTV camera above the department steps. Tiggy simply laughed when I told her, her marvellous unconcern apparently unchanged.

'I suppose it might be a problem, but only because of awful busy-bodies, and they don't need to find out.'

'No they don't, but let's be careful all the same.'

'Sure. No spanking me in front of class then.'

She laughed, but I found myself glancing around to make sure nobody was within earshot. I knew for certain I couldn't call if off, but she had to learn to be more careful.

'Sh! Or I will do it, as soon as we get home.'

'Ooh, yes please!'

'Tiggy, please, we do have to be careful. Other than when we're together we should carry on as if nothing has happened.'

'I promise.'

'I wish it didn't have to be like that, but . . .'

I left my sentence unfinished, but she picked up on it.

'The world's full of people trying to tell us what to do. Why shouldn't we be with who we please? We're consenting adults, aren't we?'

'Yes, but the law is there to prevent abuses of authority.'

'Which should be for the university to decide on, if anyone. How dare some stuffed shirt tell me who I can fall in love with? And you didn't abuse your authority. I seduced you.'

'I suppose you did?'

'*Mea Culpa.* I've wanted you for so long, Hazel, but I never dared say anything, not until last night.'

It would have been so easy to take her hand, to kiss her, but not at the bus stop. I contented myself with a smile.

We were home quickly, and as we got off the bus I recognised somebody standing on the corner of the close, the pasty-faced young man who occasionally came to see Tiggy. At the sight of him she gave a tut of irritation.

'Who is that?'

'Just some guy who's been pestering me to go out with him. Hang on.'

She shot across the road, making a car brake quite hard, and as I waited for a chance to follow safely she was talking to him. I could see his face clearly, his expression stubborn and sulky, suggesting he didn't want to take no for an answer. He glanced in my direction as I started to cross the road, said something to Tiggy in an urgent hiss and began to walk away. By the time I joined her he was a good distance down the road.

'What was that all about? Would you like me to talk to him?'

'No thanks, but I suppose I'd better. I'll see you indoors.'

She ran after him as I made for the house, calling out.

'Phil, wait!'

It was as he turned, with his mouth slightly open, that I realised I'd seen him before, and not just in the distance when he'd called for Tiggy. He was the man I'd bumped into when I first went to visit Edward Davis-Brown at Merton College. Tiggy had called him Phil. If he was Phil Paddon then there was only one reason I could think of for him knowing Tiggy.

I was praying I would be wrong, and angry with myself for being suspicious, but their knowing each other was simply too coincidental. There was an uneasy feeling in the pit of my stomach as I entered the house and went to where I'd left the PhD theses on top of a bookshelf. As I opened Phil Paddon's I glanced out of the window, to see him and Tiggy in earnest conversation on the corner, and when I looked down I realised I was right.

The page I'd opened the theses at left no doubt whatsoever. It showed a series of maps of Brancaster Dunes, each one presenting a different set of data, and quite clearly the same as those Tiggy had used for her assignment. The next page was the same, and the next, every detail of her work copied. Even if he'd done it in the hope of getting her to go out with him it was bad enough, but as I glanced up again I saw her hurriedly pass across what could only have been money.

As I sat down I felt physically sick, and was desperately trying to work out where the blame lay. Tiggy was cheating, blatantly, and with the importance of her assignment to her final mark it was far more serious than if she'd been buying essays online. She would be thrown out, unquestionably. Paddon, technically, had done nothing wrong, as the work was still his and original, but I couldn't see Dr Davis-Brown taking a very happy view about it. I had done nothing wrong, so far, although it was sure to reflect badly on me, and I'd slept with Tiggy, which made matters much more difficult. What could I possibly do?

Go straight to the university office? It was the right thing to do, but if I did I could hardly ask Tiggy to cover up our affair. That would be the grossest hypocrisy when I was reporting her for plagiarism. It would have to come out, and we would both be out.

Pretend nothing had happened? It was very definitely not the right thing to do, and it was also risky. As a second year assignment Tiggy's work would never be published, but if I gave it the high mark it deserved then Dennis Woolmer was sure to want to read it. He was also sure to read Phil Paddon's thesis, or at very least the papers derived from it, and he could hardly fail to spot the resemblance. By then I would be guilty of collusion.

I could resign anyway; leave everybody else to sort out the whole sorry mess and sell my soul to the Devil if Miles still had an offer open for me. He presumably would, but I'd be going against everything I believed in, to say nothing of the fact that half my friends would never speak to me again. I couldn't do it to Tiggy anyway.

Yet whatever I did she was in trouble. My duty was to go to the office and for both of us to accept the consequence of our actions, but as I watched her walk up the path towards the front door I knew I simply could not do it. Yet I had to do something. As she came in I held up the thesis for her to see as she entered the living room. She didn't immediately realise what it was, until I spoke.

'This is Phil Paddon's PhD thesis, Tiggy. You've copied his data on Brancaster Dunes from it for your assignment, haven't you?'